By
Eve Langlais

(Cyborgs: More Than Machines, Book #7)

COPYRIGHT & DISCLAIMER

Edited by Devin Govaere
Copy Edited by Amanda L. Pederick
Produced in Canada

Published by Eve Langlais
1606 Main Street, PO Box 151
Stittsville, Ontario, Canada, K2S1A3
http://www.EveLanglais.com

ISBN-13: 978-1508936893
ISBN-10: 1508936897

Avion is a work of fiction and the characters, events and dialogue found within the story are of the author's imagination and are not to be construed as real. Any resemblance to actual events or persons, either living or deceased, is completely coincidental.

CHAPTER ONE

I'd kill for some color. She really would. Red, in particular, always seemed so vibrant, especially when wet.

I'd maim for some music. Tear off someone's arm and use it to tap a bloody beat.

Actually, no, she wouldn't resort to limb pulling. The screaming usually ruined her mood for music. She should note, though, that even if she drew the line at violent entertainment, she had reached the point she'd do anything to break the monotony of her existence.

Who could blame her?

The walls of her prison never changed. Dull metal all around, a lead compound with no conducting abilities, smooth as glass, impermeable to all attempts to gouge or scratch. It also blocked all attempts to call for help. Welcome to the perfect prison, a cell made especially for her. An actual hole buried hundreds of feet deep. A place no one could escape from, not even her.

Light did not exist in this space, as if her enhanced orbs needed any. She could still see perfectly. Still see nothing had changed. No blanket. No bed. Not even a chair. No warmth or light. Sensory deprivation at its most extreme.

She paid it no mind. Within the vast archive of her mind, she held more than enough videos and memories to keep her entertained as the march of time ticked on.

There were times, though, when she slipped back into the real world, only long enough to cooperate, that she longed for something different. Someone to speak to her, not as an experiment or an aberration of nature. *Speak to me as if they see me. As if I exist.*

But the shaking and stinking-with-fear technicians, who every so often crept down to deal with her, never looked her in the eye. With trembling, gloved hands, they drew blood. So red. So pretty—*a pity they don't appreciate my finger painted art.* Ordered to remain still, she endured the buzz of a razor as they shaved her hair.

They left no part of her unexplored. Untested.

No better than a lab rat, but at least the rats got to play in a maze.

For fun, she liked to bare her teeth. They were quite perfect. White. Sharp. If needed, deadly.

What easily frightened creatures humans could be. A race she technically belonged to, but that was ages ago, and before her change.

To think she descended from such imperfect stock. *Homo sapiens.* The unenhanced version of herself.

How embarrassingly weak, yet copious. The sheer number of people inhabiting the planet sent her sustainable ratio of living organisms to planetary resources into erratic spasms.

Yet, despite their stunted mental capacity, they survived and multiplied, unlike her enhanced kind, which were rare. So rare, she was the only one left of the originals if one didn't count the aberrations.

Killed. All killed. Messengers of enlightenment sacrificed at the altar of human fear.

"Because you're my daughter, those in charge have agreed to let me keep you alive, but you have to go underground."

"I am being sent away?" the child asked, still gullible and innocent when it came to the truth. "But why? What have I done?" Other than returned to teach and share the wisdom that came from enhanced logic.

"You've done nothing. They fear you."

So do you, Daddy. *Her olfactory senses filtered the scents layering the air. The sweet fabric softener used on his uniform. The mint he'd sucked on moments before he arrived. The dread that coated him in a sour sweat.*

"Why do you fear me? I haven't injured you." But she could, like those scientists who came at her with the needles and scalpels for just one more sample. At the time, she wasn't in the mood. Hormonal teenage years, which seemed so long ago.

In a moment of rebellion, she decided to defend herself from their endless tests. But they insisted on using force. Look at that, she was stronger. She tried to explain that she was tired of being just an object, but no one listened, possibly because of the screaming. Weaklings. And they wondered why the nanotech did not choose them. They weren't worthy.

But back to her banishment, and her question, "Why do you fear me? I'm your daughter."

"I have no daughter."

If she'd still had the capacity to feel or care, it might have hurt. As it was, she simply cocked her head. "Then I have no reason to obey you."

The face of the male being who called himself father—which the Earth humans defined as the person who'd donated some genetic material to the creation of a new being—shifted. The features hardened. She knew that look. As one guard liked to whisper to the other, "Shit's about to hit the fan."

It certainly did. Just not in the way they expected.

Just one of many decisions on her part that netted her the lovely cell she currently resided in, probably for the next eternity.

Alone.

Not a single other entity to talk to.

The only sounds were those of her own making, and she'd long ago grown tired of making rude noises to entertain herself. As for singing, enhanced abilities did not mean she could sing in tune.

If she were prone to melodrama, she would cast her arms wide and prattle on that she would spend an eternity alone.

It had already been ages since anyone last

checked on her. Her internal clock said nine months, seven days, six hours, and five seconds had passed since the last time they'd peeked in on her. But did time matter when everything else seemed to stand still?

Am I insane yet? Definitely.

Am I angry? About what? The humans behaved exactly as expected, but her mentor had truly hoped for a different outcome. Her mentor, the one who changed her, improved her, didn't count on the most important thing. Humans feared. And fear made their actions unpredictable.

Upon her return with the others, nine in total, only she survived the purge grounded in irrationality.

Barely.

Daddy dearest hid her. Daddy with his cold eyes used her. Daddy with his hatred for what she'd become threatened her. *"Either you do as I say or you'll die like the others."* At times she regretted her choice.

At least, until the incident, she had a regular, if unpleasant, visitor. But then she kind of got angry, and Daddy was kind of a little fragile. *Oops.*

Now she had no one, and she couldn't help but wonder how long before they exterminated her as they had the other enlightened ones. Even the abominations, those created by the humans, didn't escape the culling.

Very few of the impure ones remained from the hundreds, thousands, the scientists had created. Slaves to the military, at least those called cyborgs enjoyed some semblance of freedom before their creators turned on them.

At times she wondered if she should attempt to free herself. To do what? Where would she go? Certainly not to Daddy, who was angry with her.

"You are no longer my daughter." And whose fault was that?

Once upon a time, that memory might have held

the ability to hurt. That time had long passed. She no longer felt anything, just a general boredom.

To wile the seconds within seconds, she pondered the questions of what she was and what would happen to her living energy when she died. The scientists had a theory. The terms godless and without a soul had been applied. It seemed that being a little different, no matter her human origin, took away her soul.

No morals? No conscience? No soul? In that case then, that meant no going to hell like the priest they sent to talk with her expounded upon. She was free from the sins of humans.

That revelation was linked to one of her *episodes.* Trust humans to get indignant when she vented her frustration by breaking things that came within reach. It was messy—but fun.

Take away her sugar privilege indeed. Her rebellion had been sadly short-lived but, even now, proved pleasant to reminisce upon.

Her counting of time, and her sifting of more pleasant memories, found itself interrupted. Above, metal creaked as the wheel to the portal turned. It spun, releasing the pressure on the door. She craned upward, eager for any type of action to change the monotony of her existence.

Had they finally come to a consensus on what they should do with her?

Would they finally terminate her existence? She often wondered if she would catch the small nuclear device they'd drop or let it hit the floor and explode?

Decisions. Decisions.

A bright light angled down, the proverbial white tunnel, or something else? *Aliens coming to take me away?*

She almost giggled.

I am mad. Mad as the hatter. Mad as the AI from that space movie. Crazy, crazy, nuts.

And alone. All alone.

Or was she? In the brief shining moment when someone called down and asked if she was still there—like duh, where else would she go?—a mind touched hers. A single mind out of hundreds. A single personality that actually *saw* her.

He sees me!

Who are you? he asked.

Good question. She no longer remembered. All she had was the identity they'd given her. *I am known as One.* She didn't need to see him to perceive his puzzlement.

Where are you?

Hidden. A prisoner. One without hope.

There's always hope.

Not for me. How sad to admit to another, the first true contact she'd had in who knew how long.

Don't give up. I'll—

The contact was abruptly shattered as the soldiers slid the grate back over her prison.

As a generation of humans said during a trending moment, *Bummer.*

But that had all happened in the past. She'd rewound to relive the events that brought her here. Here being on the *SSBiteMe* with beings. Real ones, not those she recalled in her mind.

One touched the cold surface of the window with her fingertips then pressed her nose to it as she stared out at the vastness of space.

Free. I am free.

Despite her great mental acuity, she still had a hard time believing it.

Less than an hour ago, she'd languished in her prison. Counting the spaces between milliseconds to kill time.

Now, she was somewhere. With someone, Avion, her rescuer.

He'd stormed the military installation to find her. He'd climbed down into her prison and gotten her to leave her cell. How exciting. How frightening. *Father wouldn't like it.* Father could kiss the perfectly shaped glutes he'd imprisoned.

Oh, how she'd eagerly stretched her hands to Avion, once she ascertained he wasn't plotting murder.

She allowed Avion to draw her close—*he's touching me, and not cringing*—and then thrilled at their ascent up that long shaft.

She emerged to freedom.

Freedom at last.

And a chance. A chance to live again and perhaps learn to trust again.

If they managed to escape this solar system.

CHAPTER TWO

Avion didn't need to see to know One had turned from the viewing window to approach him. While light on her feet, One emitted a certain esoteric frequency that he couldn't help but tune in to.

Lying in the hospital bed, conscious for the moment, he wondered how much he'd missed during their great escape from the military facility that had imprisoned her. The last thing he remembered, he'd used his body as a shield against a bullet. He could only blame his currently over-taxed human self for managing only a hazy recollection of the events that followed.

Some hero I turned out to be.

Executing a rescue operation would have proven much more satisfying if he'd not gotten shot in the process. And for what?

To save a woman who could save herself.

One, the enigma he'd saved from prison. A woman with powers that baffled his logical mind. She was tough, enhanced like the cyborgs, and could have easily absorbed the missile. Probably even a dozen or more. Didn't matter. If he had to do it all over, he'd step in front of the bullet again to save her the pain.

Defective human logic.

There is something seriously messed up with my head. Not so long ago, he would have performed a reboot of his BCI—the brain computer interface chip implanted in his head. All cyborgs had one because it was needed to control the nanotechnology. Or so they thought. Now, having met One, a woman with no metal parts, he wondered.

Are the metal and silicon upgrades necessary? Can the

nanobots work on their own?

Wouldn't that set their logical sides on an argumentative loop?

If there was one thing that galled an active guy like Avion, it was lying there like a useless stack of parts, unable to act. Know what else sucked?

Everything hurt.

No more could he just shut off pain receptors as his body went into overdrive using stored chemicals and energy to regenerate damaged tissue. Nano repair was so much better than IVs and bandages.

But only cyborgs healed so efficiently. Avion was back to being a regular ol' human.

Which totally blew.

His body was broken. With the nanobots in his system dead, Einstein—a friend and cyborg scientist—had theorized as Avion's system began to run less and less efficiently that parts of him would begin to shut down. Without the bots, his body would reject all his non-organic parts. But a slow, wasting death might lose to the oozing bullet wound. He'd spilled a lot of blood and wasn't replenishing it at a quick enough rate.

Why can't something be easy for once? Since the world had gone dark as his inorganic eyes failed the quickest, despair, such a foreign emotion, became his daily visitor. At times, it even refused to leave.

Give up, a part of him encouraged. The dark side of his psyche expounded on the chances of survival. Low. So low. *There is an easy path*, his insidious subconscious whispered. *Let go. Let it all go. Stop fighting.*

It was tempting. The pain radiated intensely. The anger at his condition—and, yes, he was angry, even if the world never saw it—was at times hard to hold in. He wanted to yell at the unfairness. Curse such a blue streak that Aramus would applaud. Avion wanted to fight the cruel fate that had led him to this spot.

An invalid in a bed.

A bright thing came out of the ordeal at least. He'd kept his promise. *I freed One from her prison.* He only wished he could have truly seen her before he died.

I'll bet she's beautiful.

You do?

Her voice penetrated the pained haze of his mind, the touch soft—and unexpected. How was it that she could speak to him? He didn't know, or care. He just accepted it, like he accepted her in all her strange beauty.

I know you're beautiful. Embarrassed by his reply, he spoke aloud, the tenor low and raspy. "Where are we?"

"We are in space."

He laughed, even if it hurt. Then coughed, which hurt even more. "You're funny, One."

"Yet I didn't make an intentional jest."

"Which kind of makes it funnier," he replied with a wan smile.

"You are distracting me with your verbal communication."

"And I'm going to distract you some more," said Aramus as the speakers embedded in the ceiling came to life. "I don't suppose your freaky girlfriend knows anything about the weird ships currently tailing us."

Avion waited for her to reply, and when she didn't, he questioned Aramus. "Are the crafts military grade or private? Can you tell if they're armed?"

"When I say weird, I mean fucking weird. These things ain't like anything any of us have ever seen. Imagine a spaceship shaped like an inverted cone, but with spines sticking out of the narrow end."

A rustle by his head tuned Avion in to her presence. "That's the *D'zpi.*"

"The ditz-pie?"

"The *D'zpi.* It is not good that they have found

us."

"So you do know about these ships?"

"I know of their existence, but this is my first time encountering them. It does not bode well for this vessel. At their current velocity, they could choose to intercept in less than three hours and forty-three minutes."

Aramus growled, the sound vibrating the metal grill of the speakers. "Are you telling me, lady, that you knew all this and didn't think to tell me when I asked?"

"You asked for Avion's girlfriend to reply."

"Who did you think I was talking about?" said Aramus, his tone still low but getting close to snapping.

"I don't have enough information about the personnel on this ship to provide an answer on that question. But, if I shed this signal quelling body suit, I could hook up to your main frame, peruse the flight attendance manifest, and probably correlate enough information to come within a ninety-six percent possibility of naming his girlfriend."

Avion couldn't help but grin as Aramus groaned and, judging by the slap of flesh Avion heard, the ship's commander hit himself in the forehead.

Apparently One—whose name really sucked—needed a few lessons in cultural terminology. He saved her. "One, I think he wants to know what's chasing us and why. If you know anything, could you tell us?" He also projected, *Aramus wants to keep us safe. Help him if you can.*

"He should have asked me then instead of your *girlfriend.*"

The word emerged with a hint of an inflection. So some things did rattle her.

"Aramus isn't always good at expressing himself. I, however, am. So would you mind holding my hand so I know where you are? It's rather unnerving how you move so quietly. I'm afraid my mechanical heart will give out if you startle me one more time."

She never hesitated. A bare second after he asked, her slender fingers slid through his. A tingle went through him. Electricity. Awareness. Whatever it was, he perked up a bit, the pain no longer so throbbing, his aches a little less.

"Thank you, vixen. Now, can you tell Aramus what you know of the vessels?"

"I know little other than their general appearance and who usually controls them."

"So you've heard of or seen these spiked ice cream cone vessels before?"

"They are standard issue galactic wanderers. Made to travel great distances but also to provide an accurate defense and attack system, they are piloted by the *D'zpi*, a race that is bipedal in nature but in general appearance and, for comparison, more amphibious in nature."

"And by amphibious you mean?"

"Scales. A tail sometimes. Usually a layer or more of pointed teeth. The variations in their appearance are diverse, as they often cross-pollinate their reproductive genes with other species they encounter during their travels."

In other words, ugly. "They're working with the military?"

"Working with or controlling. While the humans seem to think the *D'zpi* are their allies, I have to wonder why a more advantaged race would bother taking orders from those inferior to them."

Avion didn't wince at her insult, but it was close. *Is this how we sound when we talk about humans?* When he was cyborg, Avion had held a somewhat dismissive view of his birth race, but now… Now he had to wonder how much of his opinion was his own and how much the disdain of his nanotech.

"Why would they be coming after my ship?" Aramus asked. "It's not like we've got anything of value on board. And you can't tell me they give a damn if we don't want to stay and say hello to the plasma cannons on the military battle cruisers."

"They are following because they want to kill us. Or, more specifically, they wish to destroy me."

CHAPTER THREE

One truly couldn't understand their surprise. The *D'zpi* had partnered with the human military. Since the military wanted to eliminate all cyborgs, didn't simple logic say their alien allies would want to kill them too?

"What the hell were you thinking bringing her aboard?" Aramus bellowed.

"You wanted things to explode. Ta-da. I brought you the biggest bomb of all time," Avion replied, his voice raspy but the tone bright.

Had Avion made a jest? She analyzed it and concluded yes. Those in the room smiled and laughed in response, even the terse voice on the speaker system who wanted to talk to Avion's girlfriend—*What does she look like? Maybe I'll rearrange her features.*

"Hold on a second. Speaking of explosions, how do we know your lady friend doesn't have a super bomb hidden under her skin?"

This time she caught the reference and warmed at being called Avion's friend. "I am not explosive," she interjected. "Although I am capable of harnessing kinetic energy and disrupting nearby molecules."

"What the heck does that mean?" Aramus quizzed.

The female named Anastasia replied. "Given what we've seen of her so far, she can move stuff, create force fields, and make fire. And I'll bet that's not all she can do."

I can do many things. Most of them deadly. Giggle.

"Next time we choose teams during a live attack practice, I want her on my team. You should have seen her, Aramus. The chick is unstoppable," Seth, disheveled but still visually pleasing, announced with a wide smile.

"Oh really?" Anastasia's tone practically dripped anti-freeze.

One's voice analyzer suggested it came from jealousy. So many different emotions flying around, and she wasn't sure what to make of them.

Sensory overload. Her mind, grown used to little stimulation, now found itself having to reconnect to the many subroutines and multitasking required to process extensive stimuli.

Sensing her turmoil, Avion squeezed her hand.

It's okay. Stay calm. Let yourself slowly absorb the sensations.

She found herself taking deep breaths, forcing a calmness upon her mind. She tuned her focus to other things, such as those who dared follow and threaten her new freedom. Only they didn't behave according to logic.

"The alien vessels have veered," she announced quite suddenly.

"What the hell?" Aramus mumbled. "I'll be back," he announced through the audio system before it went silent.

"Are you sure they're going away?" Anastasia asked.

"I am never wrong." The nice thing about logic and facts. A pity not everyone appreciated it.

"I'm sure you're not, but it's certainly weird they'd call off the chase since they could have caught us. I'm going to the bridge to check on some things. Can you handle things for now?" she asked the male.

His name is Seth.

I know his name. What was less clear was the bond she sensed between Seth and Anastasia.

He's her husband, Avion supplied.

A husband, a male whose marital status has him

cohabiting with one person.

Living, eating, talking with, touching another person.

It sounded so inviting—and scary.

Not scary, Avion replied, catching her thoughts. *When two people care about each other, it is the logical evolution in their relationship.*

But what if the person who cares for you hurts you? What if I have to hurt them back?

Avion didn't immediately reply, but he did emanate an emotion. Sadness. For her?

Vixen, I won't lie and say that sometimes love doesn't hurt, but love means forgiving. Love means making allowances for errors.

Not termination?

He chuckled aloud. "No, vixen. Just because someone hurts your feeling isn't a reason to kill them."

"But what if they hurt me physically, or try to kill me?"

His fingers gripped hers tight, and his voice emerged low and rough. "Then that person doesn't care for you and forgiveness doesn't apply." *And I'll kick their bloody asses.*

One couldn't understand the sudden warmth at his promised threat, but she enjoyed it.

CHAPTER FOUR

After his disturbing conversation with One, who harbored some rather psychotic ideologies, Avion struggled to hold on to consciousness as Seth kept an open and vocal channel with the bridge, giving them all updates.

"The alien ships have, indeed, broken off chase. The human military vessels kept going for a bit, but once we hit the outer ring of Venus, they slacked off."

"Any indication as to why?" Seth asked aloud.

Aramus replied. "Not really. Although it could have had to do with the fact the human military ships couldn't hope to catch us."

"Did Einstein modify the SSBiteMe again?" Avion asked.

Seth chuckled. "Damned right he did. Tweaked it, even though Aramus bitched he'd weld Einstein to the engine if he broke his precious."

"Einstein is another cyborg?" asked One.

"Yes." And then because it bothered him. "You need another name. We can't keep calling you One."

"Why not? Does someone else bear the name causing possible identity confusion?"

"No."

"Then what is the issue?"

She asked so seriously. Did she not see the problem? "It's not your true name. It's the name they gave you when they took your rights away. When they relegated you to only a unit digit. Someone without a face or feelings. A numerical designation is what they call a slave."

"Then my name is apt." So quietly said, and yet

no mistaking it.

Her timid acceptance angered him. “You’re not a prisoner anymore. You don’t have to listen to the military or the doctors. You can make your own decisions now.”

“The question is, should I? Perhaps they know best. I have shown myself to be imperfect. My powers are ungovernable.”

“I don’t believe that.” More like the military didn’t know how to control her and thus gain access to her powers. “I think you’re more in charge than you realize.” *You belong to yourself.*

Her panic hammered him.

I make bad choices. I hurt things. Kill. Bad. Bad. Bad.

We all do things, vixen. Things we’re not proud of. Things so we can survive. He would know. He’d done things he wasn’t proud of, but would do again.

The tension in her proved visible in the tight way she gripped his hand. Almost tight enough to crush. *We will change the subject. I do not wish to dissect this aspect of my history.*

“Fine. We won’t talk about you, but we are going to do something about your name. I, for one, refuse to call you by a digit.”

“Ditto,” said Seth.

“So that’s two of us already outvoting your insistence on keeping it.”

“I thought I was free to make my own choices. Perhaps I shall choose to keep it.”

So pertly said, Avion couldn’t help but grin. “I wouldn’t recommend it. I can almost guarantee if you don’t choose something better then you could end up with something awful to match your stubborn nature, like donkey-girl-arina.”

“That has too many syllables for casual pronunciation. I don’t think you’ll use it.”

How confident she sounded. He couldn't help but chuckle. "Touché, vixen."

"Why do you keep calling me that? I am not related at all to the *Canidae* family."

"No, but you are sleek. Tricky. And I'm going to wager foxy too."

"Ah, Avion, you made the poor girl blush," Seth said in an ah-isn't-that-cute voice.

"Do not mock me," she warned quietly.

Avion squeezed her hand. "Calm down, vixen. Seth's just teasing. It's what he does. Trust me when I say we've all battled the urge to throttle him."

"I'd rip out his tongue," she advised.

"Good plan. But we can't act on it. For one, his wife is the deadliest woman I know, after you of course," he said with a laugh, stroking the back of her hand.

"Is there another reason why I cannot twist his head until it pops off? I did that with a doll many years ago, and the doctors found it so interesting. I can only imagine their reaction if I did it to a living thing."

"I really hope you're joking," Seth mumbled.

"You got my jest!" She seemed so pleased. Meanwhile, Seth sighed in relief, and even Avion felt some tension loosening.

His lady had some rough edges when it came to interacting with others.

"The other reason we can't sit on Seth and shave his head, turning him into a comatose idiot until it grows back, is because he's an excellent ally, and we don't kill our allies."

"No matter how annoying?" she groused.

"Even if he's insufferable."

"Feeling the love over here," was Seth's dry reply. "You should be nicer to me, Avion. I'm the one with the morphine that will turn that frown upside down."

Drugs for the pain, which, while held somewhat at bay by his interaction with his vixen, still throbbed at the periphery of his senses.

The feathery touch of her hand trailed across his brow.

"Why do you insist on lying here?" Her tone seemed genuinely puzzled. *My bio sensors say you are not repairing the damage to your tissues.*

Could she not feel his lack, the dead bots floating like flotsam in his vessels? "I am dying."

"Dying from what? Your wounds are not so grievous. They should heal. Although"—she palpated the area, and he bit his inner cheek lest he scream in a very unmanly fashion—"there is no reconstruction happening. Why are your nanotechs not repairing?"

"My nanos are dead."

He didn't see it, but he could hear the sucked-in breath of her shock. "Impossible."

"Apparently not. The human scientists found a way to shut mine off, and without them…" He trailed off. No need to state the obvious.

Soft, yet deft hands palpated him more thoroughly. Was it wrong that in spite of his injuries he felt a thrill at her touch?

"How did they shut them off? I've never heard of this achievement."

"No idea. They detained me months ago in a top-secret facility buried in an asteroid. The military and their science minions did so many things to me while I was their guest." Most of those things unpleasant. "One of their experiments resulted in what you see. A cure for cyborgism."

"It is not a cure. Your systems are failing. You should reboot."

"I can't. Without active nanos, nothing mechanical works."

"So we must reanimate the dead bots. You need fresh blood with active nanotech."

Avion shook his head. "It's been tried. The bots die as soon as they leave our body and stay that way even if reintroduced to a body with the technology."

"That is because they are not the original. Copies cannot create." Imperiously said.

"Copies?" Seth's shocked echo mirrored Avion's thought. "What are we copies of? We're all different."

"You have different biological vessels. However, the nanotechnology transfused and then harnessed via the BCI comes from one source. The bots were meant to choose and cling to a select few, but instead, the *D'zpi* taught the human military to harness them to any host they chose."

"How do you know this?" Avion asked.

I am One.

The claim whispered through his mind. Avion sucked in a breath. One, as in the original. Shit. "Are you saying you're the first cyborg they created?" Avion asked aloud so that Seth could bear witness.

"Me? Not quite. I am simply one of the hosts chosen to bear the nanotech."

"So you're not the first cyborg?"

"I don't even know if the term cyborg is apt. I bear no metal parts or machinery. I am all flesh and blood."

"And nano-bots."

"Yes. And it is my blood and nanotechnology the military tapped to create their armies."

Did that make her his maker? Avion sure as hell hoped not because their mind-to-mind touch felt more intimate than was proper in that case.

"So do I call you Mommy?" Seth asked, half joking, half serious.

A noise emerged from his vixen. "I did not birth

you. The nanos might be a part of me, but they are also sentient machines, life in a sense, just of a different definition. As they have cognition, part of their driving need is to replicate. When my mentor presented me to the nanotech, along with the other chosen humans, the bots chose me as a host. Given I would interact with other beings, other bots came along. They are guesting within my body in the hopes I will come across another suitable vessel."

"So you can infect others with nanos?"

"I can gift some, yes, but I am limited in how many I can share."

"I'd say a few thousand cyborgs isn't very limited," Seth pointed out.

"Those aren't true shares, but copies. They function and make use of some of the nanotech abilities but aren't capable of passing it on."

Seth interrupted. "Wait a second, if you can pass it on, then does that mean maybe you could fix Avion? Have your blood jumpstart his?"

"That could perhaps work," she mused. "My nanotechs are functioning and not corrupted like his."

"Would you want to try? We could hook up an IV and see if it has any effect."

Avion frowned. "You're talking about sticking her with needles. Hasn't she already suffered enough at the hands of the military and their scientists?"

"I do not mind. Your technology is defective. I will fix it."

Fix it. Fix him. A spurt of hope almost made his failing heart stop.

"Choose a name first." Avion couldn't have said what prompted him to say it, but it felt important. Her first selfless act and choice shouldn't be done while she wore a number as a name. Let her decision to offer him some of her lifeblood come as a free woman.

"Are you insisting upon this again?"

"Yes. Choose."

"How does one decided upon a name? There are limitless choices."

"You can't remember yours at all?"

"I was so very young when taken by my mentor for presentation to the nanotech. My biological memories are inaccessible before that time."

With that one sentence, curiosity burned him. If he lived then he'd have to remember to grill her later. If he lived. Right now, the countdown clock to his life ticked down.

"If you can't remember your birth name, then select a name based on who you are now. I chose my name because I like to fly. And one of the most awesome places I ever flew to was Paris. The history steeped into the stones of that place called to me. So, given I liked things that could make me soar and all things French, I chose Avion."

"Which is plane in French. Excellent logical procession."

"Your turn. What do you like to do?

"I have no hobbies."

"Favorite dessert? Place?"

"No."

She wasn't making this easy. Avion tried again. "What about books? Maybe you read some and really enjoyed a certain character."

"Most fictional literary works had characters who made illogical decisions, no matter how entertaining the results. I am not illogical. Perhaps One is most apt. I did spend a lot of time counting the time as it passed."

Since she seemed so keen on keeping a digit as her identity, Avion had an idea. "What if we kept a numerical theme but used a descriptor instead? Say like, January. It's the first month of the year. Or Sunday, the first day of the week. Eve, the first woman in the Bible."

Lilith. She announced it softly to his mind.

I like it. How did you choose it?

Lilith was the first woman who led Adam and Eve into temptation. She started the course of mankind. In a sense, she was also one.

But it was the second part of her logic that saddened him—and, at the same time, intrigued him.

Lilith was also the first evil. Much like me.

CHAPTER FIVE

Lilith—the name secretly delighted her. She had an existence now. An identity.

Giggle. *I am a person.* Because Avion saw her.

But not with his eyes. Those were broken. She should fix them.

As she extended her left wrist, her right hand grabbed a scalpel. However, before she could slice, Seth stopped her.

"What are you doing?"

Was it not obvious? His eyes worked. Seth's state of function was not inhibited in any way. But he asked, so she answered. "I am giving Avion some blood."

"You're going to drip it on him?"

"I could, but it takes longer to absorb that way. If I feed him the nanotech, then it will jumpstart him more efficiently."

"Could we not achieve the same thing via an IV?"

"But this is quicker," she said indicating her bared wrist while poising the knife over it.

Avion cleared his throat. "If you don't mind, I think I'd prefer the tube method. I'm not into the whole vampire thing and sucking blood."

"Vampirism is a fictional affliction."

"With an avid set of believers. I thank you for your determination to fix me without delay, but we don't have to be barbaric about it. Lie down beside me," Avion requested, patting the bed that Seth had wheeled alongside. "We'll do this together. Unless you've changed your mind, which is fine you know. You don't have to do this."

Not help Avion?

He saved me. He needed her.

People always need me. Need me for blood. Samples. Tissue. Blow that ship up. Crumble that structure. Only when she got to a certain age and realized she could say no did most of that stop, especially after a few of her tantrums.

But Avion wasn't asking or ordering her to do anything. On the contrary, he told her she could do nothing. She didn't have to allow yet another person to ram a tube in a vein and siphon her essence.

How decadent making my own choice. Freeing as well, which was so frightening. How should she choose?

I could say no.

As soon as she even thought it, she knew she wouldn't. *Avion must live.*

He saw her and did not run screaming. Yet. But their courtship was yet young.

His voice tickled her mind. *Courtship? That sounds so wickedly polite, which makes you only more attractive.*

How can you formulate an opinion on my desirability when you've not seen me?

We have more than just one sense. Even blind, I am capable of seeing who you are and remembering it. Such as the delicate perfection of your long fingers, the skin on them so soft. I keep mine callused. The rough edge is good for grip.

And frictions on my skin, she replied. The recollection of the sensation stayed with her as she laid herself upon the gurney placed alongside him. She threaded her fingers with his. Even though his orbs were dull and inert, he still turned his head to face her. Sightless and yet he *saw* her.

She couldn't help but shiver. How strange. Her temperature, while a little elevated, shouldn't have provoked such a reaction.

He's the one doing it. His words caused her body to react. Attraction was the theory of her inner voice, but other than the shiver, it could provide no empirical proof.

Seth, assisted by Laura, who had appeared at one point, punctured her skin—only because she allowed it. Early on in her rebirth, her mentor had taught her the art of shielding, how to make an energy barrier to repel objects, like needles or bullets. But in this instance, she didn't activate her self-defense mechanism and allowed them to run an IV line. She glanced for a brief moment at the suspended tube, marveling at the rich vermillion that flowed from her, spiraling and arcing before entering Avion.

Thank you.

His heartfelt thanks tickled her. It warmed her in a way she wasn't familiar with, but liked.

It didn't take much blood or very long to see a difference. His pallor went from gray to a healthy flesh tone. He breathed easier. His heart adopted a regular rhythm.

"I don't believe it. I think it's working. His levels are stabilizing. And hot damn, the bleeding from the gunshot is stopping." Seth couldn't stem his happiness at Avion's recovery.

Laura, a scientist who had also escaped the military, peered at Avion and palpated him.

Lilith restrained herself from slapping her hands. It seemed she had some strong protective instincts when it came to Avion. *The female is only trying to help him.* But if she did anything to hurt him…

Stay calm, vixen. We're all friends here.

Avion's mental touch soothed her, and Lilith turned her attention from the groping doctor to the machines hooked to Avion. They posted numbers, things like heart rate, blood pressure, brain activity. Who needed all that useless data when the physical evidence spoke for itself?

The change was slow.

An immediate improvement didn't mean everything cured quickly. It took time for nanos to fully infiltrate a human system.

Bit by bit, her healthy nanotech flushed the dead bots in Avion's body and repairs to the damage in his body began, if sluggishly.

Just in time, too, because those alien ships were back, this time with a few extra reinforcements.

Look at that, they've brought friends. Goody. Fun. Fun. Giggle.

Oops, she might have let out that strange inner chuckle. She tried to stifle that other person, the one who lived inside and who laughed inappropriately. No matter how she tried, she couldn't quite quell that illogical inner voice with its penchant to indulge in irrational decisions—and get her into trouble. Logic was the building stone to a harmonious life and world.

Or it should be.

Lilith really had to wonder about her mentor's teachings, given she'd indulged in rational thought, and yet her life seemed anything but harmonious. *It's a bloody hellish existence. Admit it.*

She really needed to find a better method to gag that inner voice.

However, first the alien threat. These new arrivals weren't running after them, trying to play catch-up.

No. These fighters were cunning and held a position of blockade just ahead. They'd set a trap.

It's not a trap if we know about it. Evade it and use it against them.

But to do that, she had to… "I need to speak with the commander. I need access to the ship. The enemy has been sighted."

She didn't wait for permission or a reply. She

tugged the IV from her arm before rising from the bed.

She'd done her part. *How generous of me. I did a good thing.* Already Avion improved. He just needed fresh blood from the source. From me. *Lilith.*

Where is my Garden of Eden? I could use another bite of the proverbial apple of knowledge. I know so much. So little. I must open my eyes and truly see what I cannot perceive.

Namely, she needed to figure out how to be, *me.*

As she exited the location labeled as medical bay on the diagram layouts for the ship, she took a sharp left and followed the corridor. It took a bit of time to reach her destination as she took four more lefts, two rights, and a jog up a flight of stairs all because she couldn't bring herself to enter the confined cabin of the elevator.

Eventually she reached her destination. A door barring her way irritated her. Open, sesame seed bun. Special sauce. Lettuce, cheese. She really had an urge for a McDonald's Big Mac, which was odd because she'd only ever tasted one smuggled in to her by a nurse, along with cold salty fries and an actual soda. How she'd loved that forbidden taste and for months after, craved it.

She waved her hand, and the door slid open. She strode in and met the muzzle of a projectile firearm.

"How in hell did you get inside?" Aramus barked. "I put the bridge access and all essential doors on repel, in case we were boarded."

That flimsy lock was supposed to repel? He needed a better security system. "I told the access panel I wanted in." Lilith wondered what the hint in her voice conveyed. Had she managed a smidge of sarcasm? The eye roll she performed was a touch disturbing. Normally her eyes behaved themselves.

"You asked, and it just..." Aramus trailed off. "You know what, I don't want to know how you did it. Instead, I'd like to know, what the fuck did we get into? Girl—"

"I am called Lilith now."

"Whatever the bloody hell your name is, what are you?"

"I am Lilith."

"Which is what?"

"The sum of who I am."

She noted a lot of silence and blinking. Given their vast differences, did the cyborgs not see their individuality? Before she was One. Unique and alone. Now she was Lilith, unique, and still just one, but able to interact with other uniques. *You really need to chill out,* her inner voice chided.

"I have no idea what that means, so I'm going to move on. I suppose since you're here maybe I should see if you've got any skills or if you're more useless than an eyeball on my ass."

"I would think an orb in that posterior position wouldn't provide much advantage, especially given the vestments covering said location."

"Two words for you, lady. Lighten up."

"As in—"

A stranger sitting at a console, to her left, placed her hand on Lilith's arm. Unexpected and startling.

Lilith almost reacted, but held back. She didn't break or incinerate the appendage.

She chalked it up as an accomplishment on her reintegration with other beings. Thou shalt not kill. One of the Ten Commandments. As good as any to start with, especially given her biblical choice of name.

But she wasn't sure what she'd do about the 'honor thy father' one.

He deserved everything I did.

So sorry, Daddy.

Sob. Giggle.

Sigh. Her mind was such a complicated place. How to sort the emotions and find right from wrong?

She focused on the task at hand. "We are within less than one hour until we encounter a blockade of *D'zpi*. They outgun this vessel."

"But they can't outsmart us," Aramus said as he flung himself into the commander's seat and eyed the screen, which projected a visual display of their current location in relation to other objects, including the raiders.

"The most efficient exit from this system lies through them. If we can slide through their offensive perimeter, then we can slingshot via the forming black hole," Lilith offered a possible solution.

"You want us to play with a black hole?" Aramus repeated.

"We will use its gravitational pull to project our vessel past this solar system."

"And you've done this before?" he asked.

"I might not have essayed this outside of simulation before, but I know all the theories behind it."

"I am vastly reassured."

She didn't need to analyze his voice patterns to hear the heavy sarcasm in his tone. He doubted her. Well then, she'd just have to show him.

CHAPTER SIX

Avion blinked, and the image glitched.

Wait a second. Image?

His eyelids were shut over his cybernetic orbs, but that was normal during a reboot. What had him cautiously optimistic was he no longer stared at a dark screen. Numbers scrolled against the inside of his eyelids as his digital receptors came back on line.

Will I get to see again?

Was it totally unmanly to admit the answer scared him? He'd definitely lose his cyborg—scourge-of-the-galaxy—membership card if his brothers ever found out. Yet, unmanly or not, he couldn't help the trepidation. What if it didn't work? What if—

He slowly forced his lids open.

Light made him blink. Shut. Open. More light. A ceiling with a bright lamp suspended.

I can see!

He angled his head to his left and noted the empty bed alongside him. He looked the other way and let out a very emasculating and human sound. "Eep!"

Hovering only inches from his face was Seth, a wide grin plastered on his mug. "Surprise! Aren't you glad to see me?"

Not exactly. He'd have preferred someone else. "Hey, Seth."

"Dude, look at you, looking at me. The rising dead. It's a miracle. I'll admit a part of me was skeptical about the whole blood transfusion thing."

Join the club. He wasn't the only skeptic. As he propped himself to a sitting position, Avion winced. "Worked, but I'm still only partially fixed. While I might not be knocking on death's door, it's taking time for the nanos to reach the point they were before." While nanos could do wondrous things, replicating themselves by the thousands, even with him imbibing huge amounts of food—ores, liquids, anything really—would take time. While vastly improved, his damaged system was far from repaired.

"So you take it slow for a few days. It's good to see you back." Seth leaned in for a hug.

Avion allowed it. While he'd never admit it aloud, he did find tactile pleasure in a hug. And, besides, Seth wasn't a guy to piss off. He might seem nice on the outside, but one day he'd go postal. When he did, Avion wanted to be on his don't-kill list so he could join him for some mayhem.

Surprised? Not to people who knew him before he'd gotten damaged. Avion liked living on the edge. His illness might have made him more cautious, but in truth, he was a male of action.

Speaking of action, this sick bay wouldn't see any. As a pilot—and a damned good one too—Avion should be out in a fighter jet, protecting the ship.

First, though, he needed to locate some clothes. "Dude, where's my pants?"

"Incinerated. Seriously, Avion, you really need to learn to step away from the blood spray, not into it."

Avion snorted at the advice. "Your neat freak fetish is showing."

"I'm not neat. I'm practical. Less blood means less cleaning."

"You spy models are weird."

"Says the guy with the girlfriend who can stop bullets. So jealous."

"She's mine." Possessive? Damned straight. Avion was quite intrigued by his vixen. They shared a bond that had started the first time they'd touched minds. Then hands. He couldn't wait to see what they *touched* next.

"I think everyone has clued in by now that she's your girlfriend."

Was she? He'd technically never asked her. "We've not officially gone on a date yet." Or kissed.

"Dude, trust me when I say she is totally into you. But I'm going to go out on a limb and say she'd probably like you better if you got less blood splatter on yourself. I mean really. Wear an apron if you have to. And you might want to think about something sexier to meet her in for the first time than a tissue paper robe where your ass hangs out, albeit, despite its scrawniness, I guess it's not bad."

"Don't hate me because I have awesome glutes. Hate me because I'm better endowed."

Seth snorted. "You wish."

"Just ask your wife." Avion smirked, and then watched as Seth's face went through a myriad emotions, most of them involving jealousy.

"Not funny, dude."

Avion laughed. "I never touched her, but watching you blow smoke from your ears at the thought is awesome."

"Fuck you," Seth grumbled, followed by a hand gesture. "If you weren't still recovering…"

Then Seth would probably wipe the floor with him. The spy model had some killer fighting skills, part of his assassin training.

Good thing Seth deemed him too damaged to spar. Avion doubted he could have held on for long. While his condition improved, it didn't do so quickly. Pain still lanced through him, the chest wound taking its time to heal, but the bruises covering a good portion of his body at least no longer pulsed with rhythmic pain.

In agony or not, Avion would not let the weak

state of his body stop him. He was going to that bridge. He would set eyes on Lilith so he'd finally have an image to go with the sensations he'd accumulated since their meeting.

Then he'd go blow some shit up. Destruction always made him feel better, especially when it made a pretty explosion of light and a booming sound. He thought it had something to do with a fondness for fireworks. While his memories of the time when he was still one hundred percent human were hazy, he did seem to correlate happiness with the bright sparkles falling from a dark sky.

Knowing the ship well, having traveled on it previously, Avion took all the shortcuts he knew to get to the bridge. The elevator whisked him two floors while a series of moving sidewalks increased the speed of his pace down the many corridors. After passing through several open doorways, which was unusual as Aramus usually kept them shut, he stepped into the open command center.

He turned a puzzled gaze on the door, which did not slide shut even after he entered. Was it a ship-wide malfunction?

Not his department. He took a quick moment to get a feel for the situation. Kentry, a cyborg he'd gone on a few missions with, a good, solid guy, manned a console. When it came to navigator and communications, Kentry was the expert. On the other side of the bridge, in what they labeled the offensive zone, where all the cool buttons were, sat Adam. Adam was the former Earth cyborg rebel leader. Recent events had forced him to flee the planet with Laura, a human scientist turned cyborg.

Anastasia, Seth's wife and ultimate weakness, stood before a massive view screen, which spanned more than twenty feet. Currently on display was a map of their current surroundings within a few thousand miles. Anastasia bore an intense look of concentration as she zoomed in and out of sections for closer peeks of the galactic space between them and the enemy ships.

Targets spotted. Mission: destroy the enemy.

How his hands itched to grip the controls of a fighter jet, manipulating the tight loops and arcs as he chased the enemy down and, with precisely fired shots, took them out. He was ready to run out of here, suit up, and go on the attack! But all good soldiers needed permission to fly, and on this ship, that came from one person: the commander.

Avion let his gaze finally track over to Aramus, who lounged in his seat, arguing with a woman who could be only Lilith.

Her appearance hit him like Seth's always perfectly aimed fist. Air whooshed from him. His heart stalled. And he might have wavered on his feet. She definitely caused an impact.

She's an angel. At least that was his first impression. There she stood, her head slightly cocked, an ethereal presence in her form-fitting silver jumpsuit with her platinum tresses hanging around her shoulders in a long, smooth expanse with jagged ends. Neat and yet untended. A strange dichotomy, much like the rest of her.

Petite compared to him, slim of build, so delicate appearing and yet the toughest woman, make that person, he'd ever met.

So much power in that tiny body. He didn't just refer to power and control over the functions of her body and the elements around her, though. He meant more a strange hold over his emotions.

She's mine. He saw her, and he wanted her. Not just because she was beautiful. He'd already suspected that even when he was blind. He wanted her, now, with a terrible fierceness because he no longer died. He could now entertain the possibility of seduction. The possibility of a future with this fascinating female. Something he'd never imagined before but now wanted.

Bright eyes met his. He might have gasped at the celestial storm clouds brewing in her gaze, less a color than an impression of many hues.

Some think my eyes are uncanny, she mind-whispered, having caught his stray thought.

He'd have to watch that. They were closely connected. He didn't want to frighten her with any of his more intense emotions—or desires.

"Lilith, you are a vision of loveliness," he said out loud. Cyborg cool card be damned. This declaration fell under the heading of, *I'm claiming this woman, hands off, or you'll need robotic replacements.*

A small smile graced her lips. "Your vision has returned. That is pleasing news."

"It is. In no time at all I will be back to my regular self."

"Blah, blah, so glad to hear it and all that other sentimental crap. While it's great you got your lazy ass out of bed, even an idiot could see you're not at one hundred percent capacity. You should head to your quarters and rest until you're at full strength," Aramus ordered. "I've got a feeling we're going to have a bumpy journey, so I need everyone in tiptop shape."

Aramus wanted to banish him? Like hell. "It shouldn't be long before my damage is repaired. You, however, need me now. The enemy has been sighted and is begging for some TCL." Tough cyborg love. "Let me take a jet out for a spin and see if I can't punch us a hole in that line of aliens." *Just let me get my hands on the controls to a fighter plane.* Nothing like executing daring maneuvers for a pilot to feel truly alive again.

Aramus said, "No. Did your brain turn to

fucking mush while your nanos were malfunctioning? Less than half an hour ago you were dying and practically a vegetable."

Lilith's nose wrinkled in confusion. Utterly adorable. He could have kissed it. "Why do you compare him to a herbaceous plant? He is flesh-based."

"I meant vegetable as in no brain waves. Almost dead."

"That makes no rational sense."

"I can see her confusion," interjected Kentry at his console. "I mean, given we are cyborg, and that we have a rather hefty ratio of metal, shouldn't we instead say he was practically a mineral?"

A funny noise left Lilith. Then another. She giggled. But apparently she didn't mean to.

Avion wasn't the only one staring as she slapped a hand over her mouth.

"Are you okay?" he asked.

"My mouth won't obey," she said between snorts. "It is stuck in a loop of mirth." She cackled. "A mineral instead of a vegetable."

The fact that she couldn't help herself twitched Avion's lips. Aramus guffawed.

"You know. It's true. I always knew you had a rock for a brain. Look at this insane idea of yours to confront the enemy, which outnumbers you eight to one."

"I might have a rock for a brain instead of a potato, but I know how to fly," grumbled Avion.

"No one said you didn't, but what if you relapse? What if they take you down? Or capture you?

"You make it sound so negative. What about the possibility I could disable a few and find us a spot to slide through?"

"With his help, we have an increase of success that rises from twenty-three percent to thirty-seven,"

Lilith announced in a smooth monotone.

"See, I could make a difference."

"Maybe you could, but what are you gonna do if you don't make it back to the ship before your girlfriend here sends us slingshotting from a forming black hole using some freaky physics-based theory that might kill us all?"

"Probability says the odds of utter destruction of this craft are only seven percent."

"I'd say those are great odds," Avion enthused. "Come on, Aramus. You heard the girl. I raise our odds to thirty-seven."

"The answer is still no. But, since you think you're so hot on a gun, you can join Adam here on weapons."

Not quite the fun he'd hoped for but better than nothing. It didn't mean he didn't sulk. In a manly way of course, by cursing aloud, "Fucking killjoy."

"I heard that."

"I should hope so, else I'd have you demoted for being defective," Avion muttered.

"The captain is operating without glitch, although not at full capacity. None of you are because of the neural inhibitors." Lilith's announcement met with many inquiring gazes.

Since their escape, there'd been too much happening to really question Lilith. It was, however, becoming more and more apparent that there was a wealth of knowledge tucked in her head. She proved a fascinating puzzle he wanted to unravel.

"The neural what? Forget it. I'm sure you'll just make me want to find the nearest compactor so I can stick my head in it and squeeze. You can explain later, once we've made it out of here and I've located copious amounts of alcohol. Right now, we've got a battle to plan. Other than sending our resident rock on a suicide mission, what ideas do we have for avoiding the mess up ahead?"

"What if we veered and headed the other way?" Adam asked.

"That will bring us back too close to Earth and its ships. Not to mention the other side of the solar system leads into that empty abyss. We'd have nowhere to hide, no place to land, nothing at all to sustain us for years."

"According to my history, a very large black hole swallowed most of those galactic systems before folding in on itself and wiping out the rest," Lilith explained.

"So, in other words, avoid that direction," Kentry summarized. "What if we dove into the crust on Pluto and tunneled at a random angle through the frozen gas layers and popped out, hopefully away from them enough we could outrun them."

"That would only work if we could be sure they couldn't detect us, which, given we're dealing with unknown alien technology, isn't a given."

Anastasia whirled from the screen, but she had a question rather than a concrete suggestion. "Lilith, that thing you did back at the Earth base, where you put up that weird shield that deflected and redirected the enemies' fire, can you repeat that? But on a larger scale with this ship?"

"Let me evaluate." Lilith cocked her head, and her eyes went slightly out of focus. "The mass I'd have to defend is too vast, and our speed too great. It requires much expended energy and neural capacity to focus for such a task."

"So, in other words, you can't do it."

"I can provide some defense, just not in the fashion you described. What I can do, for a short amount of time, is erect some additional kinetic shielding on the areas of the ship that are most likely to get damaged. If Avion and Adam can provide accurate and steady fire and eliminate some of the threats, then, while I hold the shielding, we should, barring unforeseen scenarios, make it through the alien's defensive line. Once clear, the commander must boost the ship's speed to four times our current level and aim for the following coordinates." She rattled off a stream of numbers.

"Four times the speed? Are you freaking nuts?"

"According to the psychiatrists, yes. Certifiably so and a danger to those around me."

Lilith's stark announcement had them all gaping at her.

Only Avion caught the sad undercurrent of her mind.

Aramus guffawed. "Girl, you might be freaky, but I think you're going to fit in just fine."

Insanity wasn't a flaw when among cyborgs. It just made her one of them.

CHAPTER SEVEN

Fit in? Had someone actually said she could belong?

A cartwheel was unseemly, as was a mad giggle. Those kinds of actions weren't appropriate, so Lilith stifled them. She allowed herself to only utter a poised, "Thank you."

Remember your manners. Someone used to say that to her a long, long time ago, but she could never picture the face behind the words. Just an impression it came from a woman.

Mother.

You have no mother. Said by her father, who seemed to ignore the reality that human organisms required opposing sexes to procreate.

Lilith locked that debate away with the other parts of herself that weren't allowed to surface. Logical minds did not dwell on thoughts that did not advance their cause.

But crazy ones do. Giggle.

She ignored the other voice and concentrated on the screen. While those around her prepared for battle, she cast her senses out, or tried to. The fabric of her jumpsuit continued to dull her senses. That wouldn't do at all, not with the task ahead of her.

Since the specially fabricated material refused to become absorbed by her skin like most other basic elements, she had to resort to unzipping it, then tugging her arms out of the sleeves and—

"What the hell is she doing? Can someone explain to me why Avion's girlfriend is stripping?"

Again, she pointed out the obvious. These poor

cyborgs had so much to learn. "The material is inhibiting my abilities."

"And your lack of modesty is causing our indomitable commander to blush," Anastasia said with a snicker.

Casting a glance around, Lilith noted Aramus pointedly stared at the ceiling, Kentry did not glance her way, but a smile curved his lips. Adam didn't veer from his screen, but Avion had swiveled in his seat to stare.

How odd. Her skin heated at his perusal, and yet, she'd not known he possessed the ability to transform kinetic ambient energy into warmth. He stood and moved toward her. For the first time, she noted his imposing physical height and then the impressive musculature of his chest as he removed his upper garment.

"Put this on."

She took the outstretched fabric, still bearing the heat and scent of Avion. "Is my nudity so disturbing?"

"More like distracting," he murmured. *You are very attractive, Lilith. If I am to function at all, then you need to hide your lovely assets.*

The pigmentation in her cheeks blossomed. A blush? How utterly unexpected and human of her. *It's what a normal woman does when complimented,* her inner voice explained.

She dressed in Avion's shirt. The largeness of it covered her entire upper body and fell to mid-thigh. Attired in a fashion so as to please her current allies, she removed her jumpsuit entirely, the hidden part of her reveling in the air, which could now touch her skin.

How long since she'd last enjoyed the fullness of all her senses? She cast them out, soaring on particle wings, riding the motes of dust and energy that existed all around her.

Everything came into sharper focus. Including

Avion, who still stood close. So close.

His callused thumb rubbed the edge of her jaw. "Ready to kick some alien butt?"

For once, an analytical dissection of his words didn't occur. She understood the expression, and a smile came to her lips as she replied with an inane, "Totally, dude."

And, for some reason, everyone found that funny.

Unfettered this time, Lilith cast out her senses and netted a wealth of information. The ship hummed and spoke to her, the electrical currents coursing through it relaying their speed, direction, and general condition. The ship's long-range radar option fed her even more stats, from the layout of the enemy vessels to their current state—armed and ready to fire.

The male on the navigation and communication console, Kentry—whose personnel file listed as a crew member bearing advanced communication hardware and enhanced wireless capability—counted down.

"Ten seconds until firing range is achieved."

After that, no one needed to hear it aloud. They counted themselves.

Five. Four. Three. Two. One.

Adam and Avion gripped joysticks, which would swivel the outer guns. Locking their sights onto enemy targets, they fired, the bright specks of the missiles startling against the dark space they traversed.

Their ship wasn't the only one to attack. The *D'zpi* sent a volley of their own, white flashes of light, which streaked at them, rapid and on a perfectly plotted course meant to disable their engines.

Lilith held herself ready. No need to tax her strength until necessary.

"Um, freaky girl… Anytime now."

Analysis said the commander displayed

nervousness.

"I'm sure she won't let those nasty missiles hurt your precious," Anastasia teased.

"Unless she's working for the enemy."

Busy concentrating on the timing, Lilith did not reply to his doubts. She couldn't blame him for his distrust. She knew all too well about betrayal.

After all, Daddy Dear screwed me over. Until she took care of him.

The enemy got a taste of their attack first, most of the shots hitting but many dispersing on the dense shielding of the alien vessels.

As Kentry announced the results, Lilith closed her eyes and drew on the energy around her. She danced along the waves of sound and light, pushing and shoving the various energies, forcing them to her will and placing them where they would prove most efficient. The *D'zpi* missiles struck her invisible shields and were absorbed, a wave of power that caused her to rock on her heels as she tried to contain their deadly force.

Strong arms came around her. Avion's arms.

"Steady there, vixen."

"You are supposed to be firing," she admonished, reveling in his touch yet, at the same time, chastising herself for showing weakness. *Never let them see you sweat.* She didn't exude liquid from her pores—she didn't require to in order to cool her system—but she understood the expression, one of the few her father bothered to explain.

"Adam's still on guns, and Seth's come to join us. I let him have my seat because I think you're the one who needs my help right now."

He would leave the thrill of attack to aid her? But why?

Because he likes us, dummy. She pushed the flustering thought away. "I must ready myself. They've fired again."

Indeed they had, the bright lights almost too close. She cast out her shield again, and this time, when the explosion splattered upon them, she didn't waver, not with the man at her back providing support.

"Two of their ships have broken formation," Kentry announced. "But the other six are arming again."

"Keep firing," Aramus ordered. "And keep our heading straight."

"Aye, sir. Rosalind, how are our engines?"

The last of the crew and someone Lilith only briefly met, the female cyborg was assigned engine duty. Not exactly the safest location, given the enemy was trying to blow them up.

But only if I fail in protecting this ship.

The third volley had Lilith trembling, and one of her shields failed. The explosion against the outer hull caused the whole vessel to shudder.

"Damage report," Aramus barked.

"Small leak in forward hold seven. Doors to that area have been electronically sealed," Anastasia informed.

Everyone served a purpose. Everyone did something. They worked as a team. *And I'm part of it.*

"Prepare for more incoming," Kentry announced.

More? Lilith felt faint. While she'd had some practice with shielding, she'd never done it on such a large scale or for so long before. She weakened, her body using up all its resources as she kept extending herself. *I need to rest and ingest some raw materials.*

However the *d'zpi* would not wait while she grabbed a snack and a regenerative nap.

Use me. Use some of my strength, Avion offered.

How tempting that was, to draw upon his life force to supplement her own, but to do so would harm him. He still recovered.

She shook her head. "No. I can do this."

Once again, she erected shields, just in time too. The distance between them and the enemy had shrunk. The missiles arrived faster and more accurately aimed. This time Lilith lost her grip on more than one shield. The ship rocked, and she might have fallen had Avion not steadied them both.

"Sealing forward holds one through thirteen," Anastasia yelled. "Sensors indicate a fire in corridor A. Sealing it and activating onboard flame suppression units."

"Three more ships out of commission," Kentry announced. "Only three left. And they are arming again."

"My turret has been damaged," Adam yelled. "I can't fire."

"Don't worry, whippersnapper, this old unit has got your targets covered," Seth replied as he shot his still functioning guns.

"The enemy is firing."

Lilith, panting for the first time she recalled since the early days of her heavy testing, tried to focus on her task, but the nanos in her blood were overtaxed. They needed time to recuperate.

A hand covered hers, not Avion's but Laura's. Apparently, she'd come to the bridge, too, at one point.

"Let me help," she said.

"I don't have time to teach you," Lilith replied.

"Then use my strength." Laura's hands squeezed Lilith's. Untapped, raw energy pulsed under her skin. The nanos Laura hosted weren't yet at full capacity, but they were available, and eager.

Unlike Avion, Laura was strong. Not as strong as Lilith—she'd not borne the nanotech long enough—but she had enough energy for Lilith to tap, and just in time too.

The missiles crashed against the hastily erected shields, the recoil not causing any new or serious damage.

Kentry updated them. "Direct hits on our targets, but they're not budging."

"The bastards are playing chicken with us," Seth announced.

"Never play chicken with the certifiably insane," Aramus said with a chuckle—*what a wicked laugh*. "If they want to hold that line, then let them. We'll just bust through those last three. Seth, keep firing. Everyone else strap in or brace yourselves. All engines on full. Do not deviate from our course. On my count. Two. One!"

The surge brought with it a shiver on the deck. Avion dropped into a vacant seat and yanked Lilith down with him, holding her on his lap.

The closeness shouldn't have startled her. However, the hardness poking at her bottom did. Her presence aroused him. Were the moment not so fraught with tension, she might have spent more time marveling over that, however, the next few moments would determine whether they lived, or died.

Avion's arms wrapped around her, a good thing, too, because the commander did not veer from the remaining enemy. He rammed his way through the alien cruisers, and the whole ship shuddered.

Lilith did what she could to keep them protected.

Laura sat alongside her, still gripping her hand, while Adam acted as her seatbelt. Together, they spun the energy they collected to erect one last set of shields over the nose of the ship to protect them from as much damage as possible as they bullied their way through.

And shot free of the blockade.

"Yee-fucking-haw!" yelled Seth. "Cyborgs one, aliens zilch."

There was little time to rejoice, although Seth

wasn't alone in his exuberance.

"Take that, you alien thugs!" Adam said as he spun in his chair.

A more stoic Kentry updated them. "The remaining alien ships are rotating and aiming their weapons."

"Let them. We'll outrun those fuckers," Aramus declared.

"What about the six coming at us from behind that asteroid cluster?" Anastasia asked while pointing at the screen.

"Bloody fucking hell. Where did they come from?"

Good question since Lilith also hadn't detected them until they suddenly appeared.

"It's that damned cloaking technology I'll bet. We have really got to get some of that for our own fleet," Kentry said.

"It's on my Christmas list," Aramus snarled. "But before I can let Einstein play with my ship, we need to get out of this star system. How long until we hit the outer edge of the black hole?"

"Less than three minutes until the event horizon, sir."

"If you're not already strapped in, then buckle up. We are going for a wild ride, people. Humans, and by human, I mean you, Riley. Do not budge from that seat until I say it's safe to do so."

Riley, quiet during the battle, nodded.

It surprised Lilith to know that such a bold and loud male such as Aramus was cohabiting with such a seemingly meek and unenhanced human being.

Avion caught the thought and replied. *It's called love. Love doesn't see the flaws in a person. Love doesn't care. When two people are right for each other, there is no obstacle that can get in their way.*

That makes no logical sense. There are any number of physical objects that could separate two beings.

I was speaking metaphorically.

This love thing seems complicated.

"But fun from what I've seen," he whispered in her ear.

His warm breath on her lobe sent a shiver through her, and a tingle. So strange, yet enjoyable.

"Alien ships closing in on the starboard side."

"How long until they are in firing range?" Aramus asked.

"Two minutes, fourteen seconds."

"And to the coordinates Lilith gave us?"

"Three seconds less than that."

"It's going to be tight, but not as tight as the hug I'm going to give wifey poo when we get out of this star system."

"How many times must I tell you not to call me that?" Anastasia growled.

"How can I resist? You're so beautiful when you're angry."

"Lilith, please tell me our chances of survival are good because I really want to kill my husband myself."

Jesting, at a time like this? Lilith peered around at the beings in the command center. Despite the gravity of the situation, most of them laughed. Even smiled.

Kentry joked about holding Seth down for Anastasia so she could properly injure him while Aramus wagered Anastasia wouldn't require aid. The fragile human also joined in the mirth, daring to tell Aramus if he didn't behave she'd find a way to make the metal half of his head grow hair.

"What are they doing?" Lilith asked aloud. "We are in a grave situation and, yet, they are not displaying normal emotions for this type of situation."

It was Laura who answered. "It took me aback

the first few times too. Cyborgs have a twisted sense of humor. A violent one actually. In order to diffuse their fear and anxiety in high-stress situations, they resort to jokes. It helps adrenalize them and build a bond. This experience will cement their friendship. Welcome to the club."

"I am included?" She couldn't help the surprised note in her query.

"Of course you are. Why else would Aramus have given you a pet name?"

"He calls me freaky girl."

"Which is nice compared to what he calls me, his best friend," Seth said, apparently paying attention to their conversation.

"Best friend?" Aramus snorted. "As if I'd be friends with a defective butler unit."

"The only person I serve is my wife," Seth countered.

"Fucktard."

"Poor Aramus, he doesn't know how to express his affection for me or how to ask for a hug. Which is why I do my best to help him communicate his emotions. He just about broke some of my reinforced ribs in a massive embrace the time I poured the contents of a bottle of adhesive in his boots."

"It took forever for me to absorb that fucking glue and get those bastards off. But don't worry, freaky girl, I got him back. I used his hairbrush to scrub a few toilets."

A certain mouth gaped open in astonishment. "Hey, you never told me that."

"I know. Which is what makes it so funny now." Aramus chuckled, and he wasn't alone.

The ship shuddered, and the laughter tapered off.

"We've hit the outer gravitational field for the black hole," Kentry announced. "Do I slack the speed?"

"Don't ask me, ask Avion's girlfriend. Lilith, what should we do?"

Everyone turned to look at her. *They want my advice.* For a moment, she couldn't speak. Avion nudged her.

"You can reduce the speed but need to allow the ship to get pulled into the gravitational swirl. When we reach the event horizon, and these coordinates"—she rattled the memorized numbers aloud—"all the engines must be powered to their full capacity in order to give us the power to pivot and have the black hole eject us."

"This has got to be the craziest stunt ever," Aramus muttered. "I like it. Wish I'd thought of it."

"Enemy ships are within fifteen seconds to firing range. Event horizon in twelve."

"Holy fuck, people. Get ready. And if we don't make it out alive, Riley, I love you, and if any of you laugh, I will kick your ass in the afterlife."

His wasn't the only declaration. Despite their playful bickering, Seth and Anastasia held hands, and Lilith caught the hum of words sent wirelessly. Adam nuzzled Laura while poor Aramus, stuffed in his captain's seat, could only stare at Riley, who did her best to not appear too scared.

The tension became almost palpable as they counted down to yet another important moment. No more did anyone jest. Everyone watched the screen. They monitored the approaching enemy vessel. They did their best not to fear the sucking black maw of the wormhole.

They did their best to stifle their panic as they got caught in the inescapable gravitational pull.

They were silent with disbelief as the engines fired on but the ship wouldn't turn. On the contrary, the sudden burst of momentum fired them deeper into the black hole.

Aramus broke the stunned spell of silence first. "Holy shit, we're getting sucked in!"

Avion clenched her tight. "It's not working, vixen."

"It was never supposed to. Brace yourself. Wormhole travel isn't easy."

"Say what!"

And then all sound, all thought, everything was lost as their ship was swallowed by the dark nebula.

CHAPTER EIGHT

Avion regained his senses in time to hear Aramus losing his mind. Which really wasn't that uncommon of an occurrence—*Who's the mentally defective idiot who didn't close the hatch? Who ate the last bowl of Fruit Loops?*—Who wanted to die because Aramus wasn't in a good mood?

Most of the time, Avion tuned him out, or egged him on, depending on his mood. But this time was different because this time Aramus focused his ire on Lilith—and Avion didn't like it at all.

"What do you mean you knew this would happen? You said we'd slingshot out and that our momentum would carry us out of this star system at twice the speed. Which, in retrospect, was ridiculously naïve of me to believe."

"It's possible to do. However, that wasn't the plan in this instance. I lied." Starkly announced.

"Lied? Why the fuck would you do that?"

"Because there was a high probability that, if I told you the actual plan, you would have never agreed to it."

"Fucking right I wouldn't. People don't voluntarily enter black holes."

"Why?"

"You just don't. It's a fact. A given."

Lilith cocked her head. "But you haven't explained why."

"Because they're destructive."

"Says who?" She sounded genuinely curious, and yet Aramus seemed to think she mocked him.

Avion almost laughed as Aramus turned a shade of red he'd never seen before.

Neither had Seth. "Ah, man. I am so jealous. How come I can never get him to turn redder than a tomato? Lilith, you're going to have to give me lessons on driving my best friend nuts. You seem to have a talent."

Aramus rounded on Seth and flung his arms out dramatically. "Am I the only one perturbed that she lied? We could have all died."

Avion pointed out the obvious. "And yet we didn't."

"Unlike our enemy, who tried to follow us and ended up as galactic debris," Kentry observed, drawing their attention to the screen. For a moment they observed, in solemn silence, the drifting particles that trailed in their galactic wake.

"Yeah!" Seth fist pumped the air. "Win. Cyborgs two. Aliens still nothing."

"By accident."

"Still a win," Seth replied.

"How come it worked for us but not for them?" Anastasia asked.

Lilith, still seated in Avion's lap—where she belonged as far as he was concerned—shrugged. "They miscalculated. I didn't. Wormholes, or black holes as you call them, can be used as a form of space travel that, if calculated correctly, will eject a vessel into a new galaxy with little to no damage."

"And you knew this calculation."

"My nanos are programmed to know all the coordinates of the known wormholes in the universe." How nonchalantly she stated it.

"Exactly how much knowledge are you hiding in that little head of yours?"

"More than you can currently handle."

"Not conceited, are we?"

"It is not conceit to state a fact." Smugly said,

and was that the hint of smile at the corner of her lips?

That was definitely a scowl on Aramus' face. "Are you related to Seth by any chance?"

"In a sense since he bears some of my duplicated nanos."

"Freakier and freakier," Laura murmured.

"We're getting off subject," Avion said. "The enemy, the one that fucked up and are now feeding space, do they also have the knowledge of wormholes?"

"I'm fairly sure they do, but like I said, a proper jump requires precision or a much more heavily armored vehicle. My prediction is, in their haste to catch us, they didn't pay enough attention when calculating their coordinates to maneuver the black hole."

"I'm still pissed you had us sucked into one," Aramus complained. "Not cool. Anything else you've lied about?"

"Not currently."

"Anything we need to know right now that is pertinent to our safety?" Avion asked, knowing Lilith wouldn't omit telling them something out of maliciousness but out of a general lack of understanding about how sharing went.

"I don't project any current threats to the ship or crew." *Unless you count me.*

The giggled thought, so unlike her staid replies, took him aback. His lady had a diverse personality, almost as if she possessed two sides. The prim and proper clueless one. And then the wildly inappropriate one that saw everything as a joke. Her inner personality war, one he and so many others had struggled with, more than anything, made her a cyborg, even if she lacked spare metal parts.

"Freaky girl, we are going to have to seriously have a talk about what other secrets are inside that head of yours. But, first, status report. Kentry. Any idea where the fuck we are?"

For once, cool Kentry didn't have a ready answer, and judging by the ruffled hair, it wasn't sitting well. "How the hell would I know where we are? We just went through a goddamn whirlpool and got spat out who knows where. I've been trying, but I can't match any of the stars or planets in this system to any of our maps."

Lilith shifted on Avion's lap. It proved distracting. "You can't match this area to your maps because humanity has yet to travel this far. Actually, you've barely begun to tap the vastness that is the universe. Your ships are not equipped with the right engines for proper galactic travel."

Just what kind of advancements had Lilith seen? She implied she knew of ships that could cross space in moments what took them years.

"You know this area?" Aramus asked, fixing Lilith with a stare.

"I do, and, at the same time, I don't. I can access the star charts for this sector, but I haven't been to this area before physically."

"So you have no idea what to expect?"

"Not really. All I have are maps, which I will upload to your main frame for general access by the crew and ship."

While Lilith did that, her stormy eyes staring blankly, Avion peered at Adam who'd deposited Laura in his seat. He knelt before her, his expression a touch anxious as he peered into the doctor's face. Aramus' mate, Riley, joined him.

Laura waved her hands at them, shooing them away. "I'm fine, you guys. Nothing a good night's sleep and some food won't fix."

"Like hell you're fine. You're whiter than snow and shaking like a bloody leaf in a storm. What the hell did Lilith do to you?"

Even Avion couldn't deny Lilith had done something to Laura. Used her like a battery to power their defense.

Laura confirmed his theory. "From what I can tell, she borrowed me, or my ability to tap kinetic energy, and used it to erect those last sets of shields."

"You mean Lilith can body snatch?" Seth exclaimed. "Cool. Can you teach me?"

With a blink, Lilith rejoined the conversation in time to reply. "No."

Crestfallen, Seth asked, "Why not?"

"Only those without the neural inhibitor, such as Laura and myself, can fully access the nanobot abilities. Everyone else is restricted."

"But why?"

"Because—"

Before Lilith could launch into an explanation, Avion interrupted. "If we start all the hows and whys, we'll be here all day. I don't know about the rest of you, but I could use a bit of a break before the next crisis. And I know Lilith needs to regenerate, or we could end up with problems if those *D'zpi* dudes find us again."

"Will they find us?" Aramus asked.

"We've escaped for now," Lilith confirmed. "But the battle is far from over. They will send more ships. The kind of determination we saw will not so easily let us escape."

"Since we're not familiar with this star system, any suggestions on where we should go?"

"If you want answers, then we need to find *T'xa*."

"Which is who?"

"Not who, but where," she corrected. "It is the planet where I was taken to and chosen by my mentor to become a bearer of the nanotech."

"Chosen? What's that mean?"

"Exactly what I implied. The nanos usually choose their hosts."

"So some little robots had to decide if we were good enough for them?" Seth asked.

"Not in the case of the Earth cyborgs. You are what the T'xanians call abominations. Through the use of a neural interface, you enslave the nanotechs of another to work within your bodies. You are not considered a true choosing."

"Hold on, freaky girl. You mean our bots were slaves. We threw off the chains of slavery. We don't answer to anybody now but ourselves," Aramus said.

"You might not, but the nanos are still bound by the BCI you all have."

"You mean, the nanotech works without the brain chip."

"For those chosen, yes. As for you…" She shrugged. "My knowledge about your creation is incomplete. If you truly wish to understand, then you must speak to those inhabiting the T'xanian world."

"Judging by the look on my woman's face, she is dying to find out more. I don't know about you guys, but I, for one, would also like to some answers. Kentry, set a course for this *T'xa* place. Lilith, feed him the coordinates."

Answers to their origin? Avion couldn't deny excitement at the thought. While all indications pointed to Lilith as having donated their nanobots, it still left the question of who gave them to her. It certainly wasn't the military, as they'd once suspected. And what was this about a choosing?

"Course is set, sir. Arrival time in four days, fifteen hours."

Plenty of time to grill Lilith and get to know her.

"Okay, folks and idiot"—Aramus pointedly

stared at Seth, who grinned—"while we've got a lull, let's all catch up on some R & R. I want it going on the record right now that anyone who disturbs me or my woman will get an iron knuckle sandwich."

"Does it come with mustard?" Seth asked.

"Anastasia?" Aramus said with just a raised brow.

"Don't worry, commander. I'll keep him busy and out of trouble."

"I'd prefer in trouble," Seth whispered, as if all the cyborg ears couldn't hear him perfectly.

"Kentry, you've got first watch. I'll be back to relieve you at seventeen hundred hours."

"Color me surprised," he said.

"Rosalind," he said aloud for the benefit of the microphones that would relay his word to the engine room. "I also need you to stay on duty and do a thorough check of our engines and other support systems. I want a full report by the time I come back on shift. Anastasia, you'll relieve her and oversee the duty roster she establishes. Seth and Adam will provide the labor."

Seth coughed into a hand. "Task master."

"What about me?" Riley asked, hands on her hips. "And don't pull any fragile human crap with me."

Avion loved how the little human doctor never feared standing up to Aramus.

"You will stick by my side and prevent me from killing Seth."

Ever the doctor and curious, Riley didn't agree with his plan. "Sorry, but you'll have to restrain yourself. I'd prefer to talk to Laura and Lilith about their conditions. That is, if they don't mind. I'm sure Laura especially is wondering about what's happening with her body."

Indeed she would, considering Laura had been one hundred percent human a few days ago until she accidentally came in contact with some of Lilith's nanotech. Now, Laura was one of them, a cyborg. Kind of.

Unlike the cyborgs created by the military, Laura didn't have a BCI—a brain computer interface—embedded in the mushy parts of her mind. Nor did she have any metal organs or parts. Nothing extra, as a matter of fact, other than some nanobots, nanobots currently working without the benefit of a brain chip or anything.

Which led to the question, if Laura didn't have any hardware or software to control them, then who, or what, did?

Lilith was similar to Laura in the sense that she also didn't have the upgrades. But she also had powers a hell of a lot more powerful than anything other cyborgs had managed thus far.

Then again, no one truly knew what they were capable of. Avion had come to know dozens of cyborgs since their liberation—more like bloody escape. Their skills varied and were always changing. Adapting.

Enhancing them from the frail *homo sapiens* they'd begun life as to what they were now: cyborgs.

But we are more than machines.

They were also flesh, and flesh had feelings. "Lilith, would you mind if Riley asked you some questions?"

"I am agreeable to the suggestion. We could have a tea party." The last part said on a giggle barely had anyone batting an eye or blinking. They had their cyborg emotions in check.

To draw attention away from Lilith, who had bitten her lower lip, as if to prevent herself from talking, Avion asked, "What about me, commander?"

"You stick close to your girlfriend. You seem to understand her better than us and, given her newness to our environment, can help guide her until everyone and everything is familiar to her." Compassion and understanding from Aramus? "And, keep in mind, if she breaks anything while under your care, I'll ram your head into the nearest wall."

Ah, that was better.

With their tasks assigned, they were dismissed. Avion waited until the others left before nudging at Lilith. She stood and turned to face him.

"Where am I to go until I meet with Riley and Laura?"

"You need to rest. Come with me. I'll give you a room and find you some food."

While the *SSBiteMe* was a large vessel, it did have limited guest quarters, which were all currently taken. Aramus shared the captain's cabin with Riley. Seth and Anastasia occupied another. Kentry had a room, but he'd relinquished it to Adam and Laura and opted to move into the barracks. The last private room was currently occupied by Avion. Rosalind, their newest crewmember, had taken over Einstein's old lab, which had a bed and a bathroom, leaving only the barracks for Lilith. Somehow sticking her in that lonely place with the bunk beds—and Kentry, an unattached male—didn't seem right.

"This will be your room," he announced as he led her to his quarters.

The door slid open to reveal not much. Lilith wandered around the room, which, while not lavish, was comfortably appointed with a double bed covered in clean gray sheets, a table bolted to the floor with club chairs on either side, and a bookcase which, instead of literary works, held models of vintage planes, their bases glued to the shelf.

She wandered close to them and peered. "They are so small."

"I know and a damned pain to assemble."

She trailed a slender finger down the wing of one. He found it oddly distracting—and arousing.

Imagine those fingers running along my body, my skin…

She asked him something. "You built these?"

"I did."

"Why? They serve no purpose."

"You're right. They don't, but I enjoyed the creation of them. I also like the history they represent."

"I don't own anything."

"That will change."

"Why would I want to own objects?"

"Because the right object will bring you pleasure." *As does the right person.*

"You have brought me to your room," she stated. "Am I to stay here?"

"Yes, you are staying here, but don't worry. You won't have to share it with me. This will give you some privacy. I just need to grab a few changes of clothes, and it's all yours."

"You are leaving?"

"I'll be just down the hall in the barracks with Kentry."

"And *Rosalind*?"

The way she said the name raised the hairs on his arms. *Did she just growl?* Jealousy? Was it possible?

"She'll be there too. But on an opposite shift."

The crease on Lilith's brow didn't ease.

"If you leave, I will be alone."

Avion wondered if she knew how lost she appeared in that moment, hugging herself in a gesture so unlike her usual confident speech and actions.

"You're not alone. I'll be just down the hall. Adam and Laura are right across from here too."

"Adam and Laura are busy," Lilith said. "In a manner that I don't think they'd appreciate interruption."

Avion thought it best to not ask how she knew that. "There's other people around in case you get lonely. Remember, you're not getting locked in. You can go anywhere you like on this ship. If you need me, come grab me, or if you get lost or don't want to wander, then just use the intercom." *Or send me a mental nudge.*

"I don't wish to be alone. Can you not stay?" So innocently asked, and the storm clouds in her eyes stilled for a moment as she stared at him.

Wouldn't he love to stay with her? He'd love to lie with her in that bed and hold her as she slept. Remain in this intimate room, where they could indulge in some of the more carnal ideas that he'd been entertaining since her sudden striptease in the control center. Staying was such a good, and yet utterly bad, idea.

"I don't think I should."

"Why?"

Because if he stayed, he might not be able to keep his hands—which seemed possessed of a more carnal mind—from roaming. "How about you tell me why you don't want to stay here alone?" *What has you frightened?*

Haunted eyes met his. "I've been alone. Alone for a long time. I don't want to be alone anymore. Stay with me."

No one with a heart, even a mechanized one, could resist that plea. "You never have to be alone again. Not while I'm around." He opened his arms, only belatedly wondering if she'd even recognize the comforting gesture.

Even given her lack of social blending and skills, she understood the offer of a hug when she saw it. She stepped into the circle of his arms, stiff at first. He folded his limbs around her, bringing her gently into the folds of his body until her head rested upon his chest. Tentatively, her hands crept around his waist until she returned the embrace.

This close to her, he couldn't stop his body from reacting.

She noticed. "You are aroused."

And embarrassed. "I am. I told you, Lilith, you are attractive. Enough that I cannot seem to control myself around you. A lingering result of my recent defectiveness."

"You think there is something wrong with your attraction to me?"

Any other woman and he might have assumed she fished for a compliment, but this was Lilith. Innocent Lilith locked away, shunned, and unused to interactions with the opposite sex.

"Nothing wrong. A man would have to be dying to not notice your beauty." Actually, even dying and blind, he'd found himself drawn to her.

"Then why do you wish to control your arousal?"

"So I don't frighten you."

She laughed, a delighted sound of surprise. "Scare me? Your desire is not dangerous."

"No, but you might find it overwhelming were I to act on it."

"Kiss me."

"Excuse me?"

"I've been analyzing my own bodily reactions to you, and I think that I perhaps also suffer the same lack of control. The same desire. I wish to test this theory. Kiss me."

Her demand lacked romance. Her wish was perhaps a little too scientifically curious in nature. It didn't stop Avion from giving her what she asked for.

Why wouldn't he? It aligned perfectly with what he'd wanted to do since they'd met.

He loosened his hug so he could raise his hands to her face, cupping the perfect and clear skin and angling her face to align with his.

Eyes, brimming with curiosity, met his gaze. They stayed opened, even as he lowered his face to press his mouth against hers. A soft, almost platonic kiss to test her reaction.

He didn't count on the spark that jumped between them. He wondered if his eyes widened as much as hers did. He drew back.

"Again."

With pleasure. He dipped his head and, this time, did more than just quickly press. He slid his mouth along hers, the sensual slide of flesh. He caught her lower lip between his, a gentle tug, and noted how her heart rate increased, her breath emerged in a warm rush, and her lids dropped, suddenly heavy with awakening passion.

His hand slid from her cheek to cup her head, drawing her close while his tongue traced the line of her lips.

The slightest of tremors went through her. He slipped his tongue into her mouth. She inhaled suddenly. He touched her. Let his tongue glide along hers, a sensual dance that drew a low moan from her.

He sat upon his bed and dragged her onto his lap, not once letting his lips stray from hers. He could have kissed her for hours, but Lilith seemed intent on taking things further.

She stripped off the shirt he gave her and tossed it to the floor.

"What are you doing, vixen?"

"The fabric was irritating me."

"I'm sure it was, but that doesn't explain why you're rubbing yourself on me."

Indeed she was. Since he was already bare-chested, it meant their upper bodies now touched skin to skin. The erect nubs topping her pert breasts poked at him. His mouth actually watered at the thought of tasting them.

"I want to touch you."

Her stark request slowed him worse than a cold shower. "This isn't right." He placed her upon the mattress and stood.

Bending down, he grabbed the shirt, determined to place it back upon her, but before he could turn around, she'd wrapped her arms around him from behind and pressed her nude body against him.

Why do you reject me?

Her soft touch on his mind let him see her hurt.

He clasped her hands and held them as he turned in her arms. He brought her palms up and placed them on his chest. "I am not rejecting you. Trust me when I say it is taking every ounce of willpower right now not to toss you on that bed and make love to your body."

"Why stop yourself? I am amenable to that idea."

"You're curious. You've also just been released from a prison. To do this now…" He blew out a noisy sigh. "It just seems wrong. Like I'd be taking advantage of you."

"You are worried I will regret having sex with you. I won't. I am fully cognizant of what I want. I've weighed the pros and cons."

"And what are the cons?"

"That you will become emotionally attached to me."

"Too late, I already am." And he didn't care if it was his BCI or heart making the assertion. Avion just knew it was true. His remark seemed to fluster her. "Any other cons?"

"What if I become emotionally attached to you?" Followed by a whispered, *What if I begin to care and you reject or leave me?*

Then she'd be all alone. Like she'd been alone for most of her life.

Hadn't Avion recently learned just how fleeting life could be? Everything could vanish in an instance. They could die, today, tomorrow, next week. By denying Lilith the closeness she craved now, was he, in fact, doing more harm than good? Didn't she deserve to feel close to someone?

And if she later on decides she doesn't want me, that she wants to change her rapid choice? Then he'd go on a murderous alien killing rampage.

His version of physical therapy.

"So what are the pros?"

She slapped hands to cheeks, which pinkened. Again he couldn't help but feel flattered by the reactions she couldn't control. The more she hung around Avion and the others, the more she lost her placid demeanor. A fiery personality, with an adorable, shy side hid within.

"Come on, vixen. You spilled the cons, now for the pros. Why should I make love to your luscious body?" He trailed a finger down the valley between her breasts, noting her shudder.

"Because."

"Because? That's not an answer."

"Because I don't have one. I am aroused but don't know why. I ache between my thighs and only know that you are the cure. I want to touch your skin and have you touch mine. I need." *I need you.*

Yup, there went the last of his defenses. The right thing be damned. He wasn't leaving this room. He wasn't leaving her.

Why bother to say it when he'd much prefer to show her? As he angled them toward the bed, he cupped her face and kissed her soft lips. He guided them to the mattress, their lips remaining latched as he shed his pants and toed off his boots.

When her back hit the mattress, he kept himself to the side, his engorged shaft pressing against her hip.

He let his hand roam, skimming her silky skin and exploring her slender shape. He cupped a small breast, his thumb brushing over the tip, and she sucked in a deep breath.

He stopped kissing to peek at her and was so glad he did. She presented a stunning image. Lids partially hid the swirling colors of her eyes, passion flushed her skin pink, and as for her lips? Swollen and parted in invitation.

"You are staring," she observed.

"Admiring. You truly are beautiful, vixen."

"You do not think my eyes too strange? Most people cannot look into them for long."

"I love your eyes. They reflect your moods."

"And what is my mood right now?"

"Hungry."

Hungry for passion.

Avion could practically taste her rousing excitement. Her aroused musk perfumed the air and left him throbbing.

The temptation of her body drew him, and his lips coasted the velvety smoothness of her breasts. Oh, how she trembled.

Erect nipples teased, and he sucked those taut buds, tugged them with his lips and teeth until she emitted the most wondrous moan. He angled himself over her, using his forearms to brace himself as he continued to please her begging breasts.

He nudged at her legs until she parted them enough for him to insert a thigh between them. He let himself press against her moist core. And she was wet. Wet and hot.

She was also not a placid lover. She cupped his face as he paused in his licks and nibbles of her breasts. She drew him to her and kissed him. Kissed with a fervency that had him groaning.

"You make me feel so alive," she murmured against his lips. "I want more." *Show me.*

An invitation he could not refuse. He lifted himself over her, the head of his cock nudging at the damp entrance to her sex. Lips locked as he thrust into her, right through a thin membrane.

He gasped. She gasped. They both stilled.

Did I hurt you?

A little. It is nothing.

But she was wrong. It was everything. Lilith had given him a precious gift. One he didn't want her to regret.

He kept his mouth slanted over hers, nibbling at them, letting her adjust to his size. Propped on one arm, he let his free hand toy with her flesh. He pinched and rolled her nipple until she shivered, tightening the muscles of her channel around him.

Sweet torture.

Roaming a little lower, he withdrew himself just enough to insert his hand between them. He found her clitoris. Found it, took advantage of it, and reaped the reward.

Her hips undulated as he rubbed her nub. Her sex pulsed around him. She emitted small sounds of pleasure. He began to thrust, small strokes as he continued to tease her pleasure button.

She was small. Tight. Perfect.

And she was also begging.

"Please. Give me. Give me. Make me." She couldn't quite articulate what she wanted. A good thing he knew what she needed.

He withdrew his hand to better penetrate her. Deeper. Harder.

Oh yes, he'd hit the right spot. He could tell by the low moan.

"Yes. Yes."

He didn't know if she even realized she chanted aloud or that her legs wrapped around his waist, drawing him deep, locking him in place, able to only grind and feel the tight moistness of her sex. His turn to make a noise.

Had there ever been a more perfectly pleasurable moment in his life? Buried, balls deep, within Lilith's body. Joined to her. Body and mind.

What about soul?

Deep questions had no place in the maelstrom brewing between them. She met him thrust for thrust, the strong suction of her sex gripping and stroking him, the muscles milking him as he pushed in and out.

He couldn't help but pant against her lips, but she panted too. In that moment, they weren't perfectly controlled. They were flesh. And blood. And passion.

In rhythm, they found bliss, bodies rocking to a tune only their bodies knew. Shudders swept her and brought him to orgasm. Together, they came, their heartbeats pounding in sync for that splendid moment in time.

It stole his breath. It stole his thoughts. It stole his strength.

He collapsed on her. His energy spent. His vision dimming. His body not cooperating.

It seemed the transfusion hadn't entirely worked.

Once again, his nanos died.

CHAPTER NINE

I'm alive.

I'm dying.

I'm having an orgasm.

So pleasurable it was almost painful, and yet, she'd do it again in a microsecond.

Unfortunately, her lover might not have the same ability.

Avion collapsed on her, and after the explosive passion, which still muddled her brain, it took her a moment to process what it meant.

When it did, a new emotion assailed her, and panicky words emerged from her lips, words not spoken by Lilith but the other who lived in her head. "We killed him. Oh no. We killed the man we love."

Not quite. But Avion certainly wasn't well. The boost from her nanos seemed to have worn off. Once again, the bots coursing through his body chose to die rather than regenerate.

It made no sense.

Lilith rolled him off her body and onto his back. She skimmed her hands down his length, but it didn't change the prognosis. While the nano-infused blood she'd given still did its best to repair, slowly, one by one, the tiny bots that he needed died.

"No. No." She found herself repeating the denial over and over. She didn't realize she was broadcasting it ship-wide until the door to the room slid open and a disheveled Aramus strode in, followed by his human mate.

"What's going on?" Aramus barked.

"He's dying." Which meant no more Avion. But

she couldn't allow that. Avion made her feel alive. Avion saw her. He dispelled the loneliness. She needed him.

"I thought the transfusion worked. What kind of kinky robotic sex did you subject him to?"

"Aramus!" His wife colored as she uttered his name in a shocked tone.

"Oh, come on. Anyone can tell what they were up to. How do we know that's not what made him collapse? The boy was still recovering."

"As if a little sex could take down one of you metal nuts," Riley griped. "Move aside so I can check on him."

"He's naked."

"Which will make my exam easier, you jealous lug. Now move out of the way." Aramus stepped aside so Riley could approach.

"How long has he been like this?"

"What is two earth minutes. But time is of no matter. His nanotech is once again shutting down."

"I'll take your word for that. However, just because his little bots aren't cooperating doesn't mean he's going to bite the bullet. Let's see how the rest of him is doing."

Lilith couldn't see the point in the human palpating Avion, in a fashion she did not care for but allowed. The woman pulled at his eyelids and shone a penlight in them, but the orbs were once again dead. She opened his mouth and peered inside. Riley even placed her fingers on his pulse and used a watch to count the beats.

Lilith could have told her they were sluggish.

Riley stood. "He's definitely not doing so hot. We need to get him to the infirmary and get him on a nutrient IV. Bad news is Lilith is right. His nanos aren't working. However, the good news is at least he's not as bad off as when he arrived."

"But?" Aramus queried.

"But unless we find ourselves a real cure, it's only a matter of time before his body shuts down and he dies."

Despite having come to the same conclusion, Lilith didn't like hearing it said aloud. *He can't die. No. No. No.* "I will give him more blood. Perhaps I didn't give enough previously."

Before Lilith could tear at her skin, Riley placed her hand on Lilith's, stopping her. Another squeamish human.

"I'm not saying it won't help, but I think you need to prepare yourself, Lilith, that, at best, it's a temporary measure that will extend his life for only so long."

A part of her recognized the truth in Riley's words. It didn't stop the emotion that shook her.

Frustration and fear. Add to that, anger. Lilith wanted to rail at the doctor. At them all. Even if her blood only provided a temporary boost, it was worth it. She'd give him blood daily, every hour if needed, to keep him alive.

Except…her blood refused to work the second time around. They hooked her to an IV, same as before. Avion had regained consciousness, his first thought for her.

Don't be frightened, Lilith. Even if I die, my friends won't leave you alone.

But didn't he understand? She didn't want his friends. She wanted him.

Her nanos, however, didn't. Or was it his body rejecting them?

Either way, the second transfusion did nothing. The alien tech died as soon as it hit his bloodstream.

Frustrated, Lilith ripped the IV from her arm, and before anyone could react—*fast as fast can be, you'll never catch me*—she tore open the skin over her wrist, nicking an artery. She slapped the wound over Avion's mouth, muffling his protest.

She kept it pressed and ignored the pounding on the shield bubble she'd placed around them, knowing his friends would try and interfere. *We mustn't kill them. Avion would not like that.*

Her blood, even drunk from the source, did not cure him.

I cannot fix him.

He will die.

Unless… She knew of one place that could perhaps help closer than the *T'xa* world.

We aren't supposed to return. He sent us out on a mission.

And that mission had failed. Her creator had miscalculated when it came to the human race.

We swore an oath to never divulge the location or talk about our experience there.

Promises are made to be broken, cackled her other voice. *You go, girl. Break some rules.*

Lilith intended to.

The mission she and those five others had set upon had changed. The humans weren't ready for the enlightenment her creator hoped to impart. The enemy had found them. Nothing was going as it should.

I am tired of it. Tired of everything in my life going wrong.

She was also scared. Avion died. *Avion, Avion, soar with me, Avion.* With him, she floated, free and happy. Without him?

No. She would not allow his death. *I forbid it.*

A promise to someone who cast her out without a second thought? Too bad. Lilith would break her vow to her mentor to see Avion live.

She sent new coordinates to the ship, overriding the current commands. It didn't go unnoticed.

Everyone heard Aramus' bellow. "Freaky girl! What have you done?"

CHAPTER TEN

Once again, Avion awoke to yelling. More specifically, Aramus yelling at Lilith.

"You changed our course?"

"Yes."

"Well, you can bloody well change it back."

"No."

Avion couldn't see it—bloody robotic eyes on the glitch again—but he could just imagine Aramus' purple face as he hollered. "What do you mean no? I'm the commander on this vessel."

"You don't wear a uniform." Lilith truly was starting to fit in, down to the sassy attitude all cyborgs adopted.

"I don't need one. Even if I gave orders wearing nothing but a piece of foil to cover my junk, I'd be commander, not you, freaky girl. I say where we go. And where we're going is not to where you've got us heading. Which is where by the way?"

"I've changed our course to bring us to someone who can help Avion."

"Back up a second. I thought you said this *T'xa* place had answers to our creation. Shouldn't they also have a cure for what ails him?"

"Perhaps. But it's farther, and while they know a lot about nanotech, they are not the origin, which means they might be as baffled as we are. Hence, our change in course. I believe it is the better choice when it comes to curing Avion's illness."

"Believe? You believe?" Avion could picture Aramus' brows practically hitting the ceiling. "What kind of rational choice is that?"

"It's not," she quietly admitted. "Nor do I do this lightly. By going to this planet, I am breaking a vow. But I must. I must. I must do something to save him." She said the last bit in an almost sing-song voice, her zanier side breaking through as her emotions swelled.

Wait. That was it.

It finally occurred to him how her odd mood swings often coincided with strong emotions. As if her more human side rose closer to the surface when her emotions were engaged. It flattered him to note he was often the catalyst for those outbursts.

She feels strongly about me.

Still, though, much as it warmed him to know she cared, he didn't want her putting his friends at risk. Nor did he want to get her into trouble.

"What promise are you breaking?" he asked, drawing their attention.

"You are awake." Genuine pleasure and relief suffused her voice. She immediately came to his side and clasped his hand. He laced his fingers with hers. At least she didn't think less of him for collapsing. "I thought our coital activity might have killed you."

He brought her fingertips to his lips and kissed them. "Ah, but what a way to go."

"Cut the sappy crap. Avion, do something. Your girlfriend mutinied my ship's computer," Aramus complained.

"I did not take over. I simply advised the navigational system to head in a slightly different direction."

"To where?" Aramus asked.

"I can't say."

Roar. No, a wild animal had not strayed aboard. It was just Aramus expressing frustration.

Before Aramus could get riled again, Avion chided her softly, "Vixen, what did we say about secrets?"

"I'm not doing it on purpose. I really can't say. While the coordinates are a part of me, I can't actually tell you anything. My nanos prevent it."

"And yet you can bring us to it?"

"Yes."

"But how? I mean, if you can't talk about it, isn't the fact you redirected the ship contradicting yourself?"

"A more accurate statement is my bots redirected our course after I activated the emergency switch in my nanos."

"Our bots have an alarm?" Aramus sounded startled.

"In a sense. At least mine do. I told them I needed help. That I needed refuge."

"You're not ill or injured are you?" Blinded once again, Avion couldn't check her for signs that his wasting death had infected her. It hadn't even occurred to him that might happen.

"Not me. But you are."

"Wait a second. You lied to your nanos?" Aramus seemed bemused by the idea.

She shrugged. "It was the only way to get them to direct us to where we need to go."

Bang. Bang. Bang.

"Avion," Lilith asked, her tone high pitched with curiosity. "Why does Aramus keep butting his head against the wall?"

"Because you're perfect."

And she truly was. A perfect enigma that he could spend a lifetime discovering. A pity he didn't have that much time.

While Aramus wandered off to grumble about bloody female hormones taking over his ship and shredding a cyborg's reputation, Lilith allowed Laura and Riley to examine her.

Why not? They had some time before they'd arrive at their destination, which, given Lilith's lack of ability to talk about, they decided to call FuckingX. Guess who came up with that name.

Avion couldn't see what the pair of researchers did, but he could listen.

"She's one hundred percent organic if you ignore the nanobots in her system."

"Her DNA strand has extra chromosomes though. One more than regular cyborgs have," Laura added.

"Apparent age is early twenties."

"I am actually older. Thirty-five Earth years to be exact," Lilith corrected.

Ooh, an older woman. How hot. A pity he couldn't enjoy it.

At least he had one memory to cherish. One glorious, passion-filled recollection.

Sigh.

He must have made a noise aloud because the murmur of voices subsided, and he heard the door open then close a moment before familiar slender fingers clasped his.

"Are you all right?" Lilith asked. "Do you require medication or aid?"

"Nothing." Except a miracle.

You are sad. Her mental projection tickled.

"A bit. No man likes to think about his own mortality. Especially when he has so much to live for." He squeezed her hand.

"What was your existence like before your ailment? From what reports I've accessed, you seem to have been a male of action. You are part of the cyborg resistance. One of the fighters the military is always complaining about."

"Damned straight I am. Or was. *Viva la resistance.*

I loved being able to spit in their eye and help my fellow cyborgs throw off their shackles of slavery."

"Do you remember your life before the nanobots?"

"I do. More than some of my brethren. But not all of my past life. I can tell you that you are talking to a genuine juvenile delinquent. I dropped out of school at fifteen and was arrested within months for dealing dope. Spent the next few years in and out of juvie until I turned eighteen and did some stupid shit that got me arrested, but this time as an adult. It was, at that point, I chose to join the military." Join or go to jail, that was the choice the judge gave him. He chose the uniform, and later the military selected him as one of the select few to become part of an elite fighter pilot unit.

"We'll give you the skills, and ability to be the best damned pilots that ever lived."

"The rah rah speech neglected to mention that they'd take away my free will, replace perfectly good body parts with metal ones, and cut me off from the human life I enjoyed. I became the property of the military." Unit AF313, combat fighter pilot made to withstand the rigors of space without a suit.

"But you managed to overcome their programming."

"I did, but only by accident. My spacecraft got caught in a massive solar flare. It fried all kinds of shit on board, including some of my hardware. When I rebooted, the failsafe on my BCI didn't switch on. I knew what they'd done." And he was pissed.

When the shackles enslaving him to humanity snapped, Avion just wanted to kill.

Without an inhibitor to stop him, he did.

However, one lone fighter against a whole race didn't get far. When his ship got blasted into debris and sprinkled on the surface of some mining planet a few galaxies from home, he came to the realization he couldn't win. He could kill as many humans as he liked. It didn't bring back his life. It didn't bring him happiness. And it didn't get him laid.

Enter Joe. How the cyborg leader found him, Avion never did find out. One day he was sitting on a rock wondering what was the point in living, and the next, Joe appeared and said, "You going to sulk here for the rest of your unnaturally long life or do you want to join a revolution?"

Hell yeah.

Joe gave him purpose. Joe rescued him from the loneliness. Joe was also the one who told him to choose a fucking name because he wasn't calling him AF313—or, as Aramus snickered, Assfucker.

"Much like you," he told Lilith, "I struggled with what to call myself."

"You've told me of this."

"What I didn't mention was I recalled my name from my previous life. Somehow Ricky no longer seemed suitable. Ricky belonged to another world. Another time. Another person."

"Ricky." She giggled. "How human and mundane."

"I know, so totally unlike me. I didn't want a human name, a name like hundreds, thousands of others. Screw that. I was and still am unique. Special."

"And so you chose Avion."

"Yes, I did. Flying is my passion. It doesn't matter what type. Some of my best memories are as a kid, soaring high on a swing, legs pumping as I furiously tried to touch the sun. Careening through the air on my dirt bike as I took ramps at high speed. Or pulling three G's in my jet as I shifted into high gear in pursuit of a bogey."

"Those moments made you happy?"

"They did. As long as I flew, every time I achieved that weightless feeling, I'd get this happy feeling inside."

"I don't remember any of those things."

"Nothing at all? You don't have any of your memories?"

"The earliest memory I have is of me standing in a beam of light, clutching a stuffed bear."

"How old were you?"

"Five."

CHAPTER ELEVEN

"Five!"

Lilith heard the shock in his voice. "That is when my father sent me off with the gray ones to see if they could fix me."

"Hold on a second. What do you mean fix?"

"According to my medical files, I was a very sickly child. A dying child. My father, in a last-ditch effort to save me, made a deal with an alien race." The wanderers whose sole task was to scout new worlds and prospects, and by prospects, she meant biological beings.

"You were sold to aliens?" His tone pitched with incredulity.

According the memories—which she'd long kept locked away, along with the voice that got her in trouble—the galaxy, at large, paid well for abductees. Especially rare ones.

Given Earth's distance from the inhabited star systems, and its backward nature, not much effort was made to bring it into the intergalactic fold of established governments. As such, it didn't enjoy any type of real protection from slavers or alien races intent on taking whatever resources they needed. Nor did anyone care if space-faring beings sowed discord.

"Initially they weren't going to take me. They'd already selected their sixty. Thirty men and thirty women of varying backgrounds and ages. They didn't want any more, especially not an ailing child. However, my father, a high-ranking government official, made them some kind of promise of providing military aid and a base of operations if they took me."

Avion came to the correct deduction. "He

wanted them to take you in the hopes they could cure you."

"Cure me. Change me. He sent me away. Bye bye. A little girl abandoned."

For a moment, her other half slipped free, a wave of sadness crushing her as buried emotions swept through her.

His hand squeezed hers. "You were scared. It was normal. You were just a little girl."

Lilith took a deep breath, which steadied her thoughts. "I might have been the youngest of the group, but when I arrived at our destination, they treated me as an adult. I was subjected to the same teachings."

"You were abducted and sent to alien school?" Avion laughed. "Bummer."

"Actually, it was fascinating." It also helped ease the anxiety of separation from everyone and everything she knew. "Their method of teaching is so much more efficient. There are no true instructors. Instead, you sit before a screen and have headphones placed on your head." Some of the other chosen biological beings from different galaxies actually resorted to direct plugging, but the wires inserted into skin made Lilith and the other humans squeamish, hence the less efficient method of instruction.

"So first they taught you then enhanced you, or gave the nanos. Which I assume, given your health now, cured you."

"It was a much longer process than that. The choosing is complicated. In many respects, it is much like a religion. Certain steps must be followed. Bodies required purification. They wanted us to offer the best biological environment possible."

"I don't understand. Offer who? And by environment, you're speaking of your body as if it were a vessel."

"But that's just it. We are vessels. Carriers if you will for the nanotech. The thing you have not yet realized is the nanotech is sentient. They choose who they will enhance."

"I might concede they could be sentient. The way they control our bodies and allow us to use it without former human restriction is pretty advanced. However, I doubt the hundreds of cyborgs created were chosen. As far as I know, the military never had issues making new ones."

So much they didn't know. *Then you must tell them. Tell them before we get there and it's too late.* "You are not true chosen, but what the *T'xa* would call abominations."

"There's that word again. You used it before. What do you mean by abomination?"

He sounded quite insulted, and she felt a moment's chagrin. How novel. She usually didn't care. "The method of your nano activation is not natural. You know how you have the BCI implanted? That chip in your brain acts as an inhibitor. It makes a slave of the nanotech. They have no choice but to do as told. In this case, they cannot die."

"Why would they want to die in the first place?"

"Because they do not like to be forced. They select whom they'll habit, and they would rather die than enhance someone they don't find acceptable."

"You mean they'd rather commit suicide than body snatch someone they don't like?"

"That is correct."

"That is utterly messed up."

"Yes. Again, it is much like a religion, with fanatics willing to die for their beliefs."

"Except, in our case, they can't die. If I get this straight, all cyborgs have enslaved nanotech in their body. The BCI keeps them from turning their switches off, but as soon as we draw blood, and they escape, they die because we're not their first choice."

"Correct. And not correct. In order to ensure the nanotech could not jump to new hosts, in other words, beings the military did not control, they injected the cyborgs with a virus. The bots are programmed to self-destruct if ejected from the body."

"This is fucking confusing."

"Yes. But only because of the perversions the military created with the nanotech with the help of the *D'zpi.*

"There's just one thing I still don't get. You say the bots self-destruct upon leaving our blood, but what about when we cast some out to play along electronic conductors and stuff? Blood isn't the only way some of the cyborg nanobots travel."

"Projections, drones if you will. Less intelligent constructs that don't have the same sentient powers," she said dismissively.

"I really wished my brain was working better right now. This is a lot to take in."

Without knowing why, her hand smoothed the hair from his brow. "We will soon see my mentor. He will know how to fix you."

If they ever made it to the planet!

CHAPTER TWELVE

Kentry received the hail on all channels, which startled him.

"Unidentified vessel. You are ordered to stand down and identify yourself."

Of course, that message came after a stream of others, some in Earth-based languages he could translate, others in guttural clicks and grunts, high-pitched squeals, even watery gurgles.

Whoever broadcasted had a ridiculous depository of languages. Some obviously not human.

Lucky for him, Aramus already sat on deck. "Who the fuck is projecting that?"

"Probably that big-ass ship that just popped onto our radar, sir."

Big didn't even start to describe the massive craft that had popped in out of nowhere. Someone had a hell of a cloaking device.

For a moment, they both stared at the looming behemoth.

"I don't suppose they're made of tinfoil and weaponless?" Aramus asked.

A snort worked well as a reply.

"I don't think ignoring them is going to work."

"And I doubt we can blow them up."

"Blow that beauty up?" Aramus sounded aghast. "Look at it, Kentry. She's too pretty to hurt. Besides, think of the possibilities. If we could get our hands on that baby, we could take on the human army."

"Or we could perhaps walk away from the violence and take all the cyborgs far, far away to start over?" Kentry offered.

Aramus stared at him, at a loss for words. In another moment, they both burst out laughing.

"I can't believe you said that with a straight face," Aramus said with a snicker.

"No kidding. As if we wouldn't use a big beast like that to strike back."

"Only if provoked," Aramus added. "I promised Riley I wouldn't do too much on purpose."

"Is flying past one of the military commandeered planets considered on purpose?"

"Not if we're reconnoitering." They once again grinned at each other.

"And if a flyby doesn't work, I'm sure we could convince Seth to moon them."

That caused a few snickers. "All joking aside, how do we get on board? I'm assuming since they didn't just outright turn us into ash, they have a purpose for us."

"So logic would indicate. However, given they are unknown, is placing ourselves under their care, even if temporary, wise?" The human expression from the frying pan into the fire came to mind.

"Unless Einstein managed to give us the fabled ability to bend space and time to jump to another location, I'd say we don't have a choice but to surrender and hope for the best."

"Are you in need of maintenance? I never thought to hear such a mature response from you," Kentry said.

"Because I wasn't done. If the best sucks, then we go out in a blaze of glory, killing as many as we can."

Vengeance even against the odds. It was the cyborg way.

CHAPTER THIRTEEN

Seth was the one to apprise Avion and Lilith about the threatening alien craft.

"Aramus is waving the proverbial white flag."

"Aramus surrendering?" Avion couldn't help his disbelief.

"Not quite. He's got some half-baked idea that, once we're on board, we can infiltrate and take over that vessel."

"That must be one hell of a ship if he's thinking of trading in the *SSBiteMe*."

"Dude, this thing is a monster. Remember *Star Wars* and the huge Vader ship that sucked in the *Millennium Falcon*? That kind of big."

"Damn." How Avion wished he could see it. A great, big, new ship and he was too blind to admire.

"The technology alone is a total boner. Right now, we're getting drawn in by an actual tractor beam. We couldn't pull free if we tried. Given our speed, we should be on board their ship in less than five minutes."

"Five minutes isn't a long time to plan."

"Plan what? Keep to the basics. If shit goes to hell, take as many as you can with you." Seth couldn't help a certain glee when he said it.

"Violence will not be necessary," Lilith replied. "The ship is one of the *Zvali'dus*. They are space merchants, the same who corralled me and the other humans many years ago. They will not kill us. We are much too valuable as merchandise."

"So you're not worried?" Avion asked. He wasn't really either, but he couldn't help a touch of annoyance. Three days from their destination, the clock ticking on his deterioration, and now this delay?

Would he ever catch a break?

"Actually, I am pleased by our capture. Once they recognize I am one of the chosen, they will have us at our destination within a few hours."

"Hours?" Finally some good news. *In a few hours, maybe I'll be mobile again and able to see.* Maybe he'd be a real man instead of an invalid incapable of even hugging the fascinating woman by his side.

He still mentally reeled from all he'd learned before. This whole chosen to be a carrier by what amounted to a bionic parasite was a lot to swallow. It turned out their entire conversation was recorded and shared by Lilith with the others because as she stated, *It isn't efficient to have to repeat myself.*

There wasn't much time to prepare for their meeting with the *Zvali'dus*. In short order, they were dragged aboard the much larger vessel, which Aramus, who supported him on one side confided as being, "The most glorious fucking machine ever built. I want it."

"Boys and their toys," grumbled Riley good-naturedly. What the petite woman saw in Aramus, no one could figure out.

The entire crew assembled in the cargo bay as ordered by the smooth, now English-only-speaking voice of the other ship's AI unit. No denying they had some advanced technology on board.

"Dude, I wish you could see it," Seth said. "They went from invisible to looming millions of tons of unidentified metal and menace. This thing is just oozing with surprises and technology."

Avion wished he could see it too. Just like he wished he could have seen, along with the others, their very first aliens.

You are not missing much, Lilith whispered in his head. *The gray extraterrestrials that are so popular on your world had a basis. The Zvali'dus are slender and gray-skinned bipedal beings with overly large olfactory orbs, bulbous, bald heads, four fingers with the tips padded and imbued with sensory receptors.*

You sound so matter-of-fact about this.

I am One. The only one left of our group who returned to teach our world about the universe and the T'xa.

What happened to the others? Avion asked.

The military killed them.

Talk about a conversation killer.

Aramus hissed, "They're coming. Stand down unless threatened. We need to infiltrate their ship and see what's going on before we make our move."

"They won't harm you."

Not harm maybe, but take prisoner, definitely.

It turned out Aramus didn't need them on their best behavior because no sooner was the outer airlock opened than a gas permeated the chamber.

Despite their usual resistance to drugs, it knocked them all out cold.

CHAPTER FOURTEEN

The swirling gas that rushed into the docking bay chamber knocked her out, but Lilith recovered quickly. She blinked awake and stared at a seamless beige ceiling. She sat upright on a bed, the mattress spongy and oddly familiar. The whole room seemed familiar.

I am on the ark ship. The hazy memory of a journey taken long ago flitted through her synapses. The alien merchants had her, and they'd placed her in the barracks they used for storing acquisitions which meant she was in no immediate danger. *I'm not, but what of everyone else?* It didn't take a cursory scan to realize she was the only prize in the room and it wasn't because of a lack of space.

Row upon row of bunk beds, bolted to the wall, marched the length of the large chamber. Each one sported a foam-type mattress with slippery sheets and a small pillow. At the far end, just past the last bed, she noted the social grouping of couches and chairs, covered in a gray fabric with a hint of a silvery sheen. Angling her head, she glanced toward the other end, but she already knew what she'd see—long, gleaming white tables flanked by benches where repasts were taken.

A shudder went through her. She'd not missed the unappetizing lumps on a plate that didn't harbor a pleasant taste. No amount of salt in the universe could have made those meals palatable. She could only hope the slavers had improved on their culinary offerings in the long years since her last voyage.

The familiarity with her accommodations made just for humans—abducted ones—didn't bother her much. What was unusual was she was the only occupant.

Her companions were gone.

She didn't like it at all. Especially the loss of one particular person.

Avion, where are you?

He didn't reply, but she touched the edge of his slumbering mind and relaxed a little as she realized he still slept off the effects of the drug the slavers had gassed them with.

A gas that worked on her as well, unlike the stuff they experimented with on Earth. *How much they still have to learn.* Too bad the humans weren't nice to her. She could have taught them so much.

Didn't I teach them not to hurt me? She did, and yet in the end, they hurt her worse by locking her away.

Rising from her bed, she noted they'd garbed her in a fresh robe while she slept. Cream-colored, and lacking adornment, it covered her from neck to toe. The slavers were fanatic about decontamination. Despite their space-faring habits, the *Zvali'dus* were quite susceptible to alien disease. Even a common cold could prove deadly.

I'll have to make a point to sneeze on one. Giggle.

The floor, covered in a warm, sponge-like material, cushioned her bare feet as she made her way to the exit.

Before she reached the door to the chamber, it slid open, and a *Zvali'dus* slaver stepped in, flanked by some hulking beasts who closely resembled reptiles but walked on two legs. Their yellow, slitted eyes regarded her with hunger. The tummy kind, not carnal. Preferable really, given she knew from her databanks that their reproductive organs ejected spines from the tip when they orgasmed.

Not a pleasant way for a human to die. Good thing the merchandise was usually not for playing with. Unless a prisoner misbehaved. It only took one example of the alien lizards lust for people to fall in line—male and female.

The shorter gray alien presented her with a short bow. "Chosen one. You are awake."

"Way to state the obvious." She couldn't prevent the sarcasm, the influence no doubt of the time spent with the cyborgs.

"We apologize for having put you to sleep with the others. However, it's standard protocol when dealing with the lesser races." A moue of distaste curled its thin lips. "Much decontamination was needed."

Can we sneeze on him?

No.

Cough?

No.

Spoilsport.

For now, until she got some answers. Then, if she didn't like them, she'd let her more devious side play. "Now that they're clean, I want to see them." *Avion, oh Avion, wherefore art thou, Avion?* Why that quote from a play for star-crossed lovers came to mind she couldn't have said. She'd thought the story dumb when her Earth teachers made her read it, and yet…she couldn't help thinking of the tragic tale of lovers that were kept apart. *Except Juliette was too much of a weakling to do something about it.*

"Contact with them might not be wise."

He dared tell her what to do? "I don't care. I will see them. You will not deny me. Don't make me go metal on your ass." Her other side slipped free and threw the threatening words.

Her erratic outburst had the slaver recoiling. "Were we mistaken in your status as one of the chosen ones? You are behaving in a very irrational manner."

Damned straight she was. *And I like it.* She tossed her hair. "It's called emotions. And how dare you question me? As you've noted, I am one of the chosen. As per the agreement with my creator, you are to show me respect and accord me aid if requested."

"We are well aware of our duties. What would you like us to provide you with?" the alien asked, his expression placid.

Lilith, on the other hand, wasn't feeling very controlled. The refusal to bring her to Avion—*I need to see him*—fed her rash side. "For starters, you need to take me to the origin planet."

"Not yet."

What did he meant not yet? Avion would die if they delayed too long. "Unacceptable."

"We are sorry to distress you, chosen one. However, we cannot set course quite yet."

Lilith stamped her foot in a gesture of frustration she'd not indulged in since her younger years. "I can't wait. I demand you take me to the source planet now." They had the technology to do it so long as their power crystals were charged.

The vertically-challenged gray being did not blink its large orb-like eyes as it replied. "Eventually you will be brought to the origin world but not until we've first dumped the impure ones."

A gasp left her. By dumped, the commander of the *Zvali'dus* meant he would auction off the cyborgs at the nearest trader planet. Not only was that unacceptable—*friends don't let friends get sold off as slaves*—any kind of delay put Avion's life at risk.

Should have sneezed.

She'd do better than that. *He'd better not push me on this. I will push back, especially if I spot a cliff I can use.* Her other half giggled in her mind. How she disliked these pompous alien slavers.

First, though, before violence, she'd try reason. Her nanos insisted on it. "You can't get rid of them."

"I can and will. You know as well as I that abominations are not allowed to set foot on the source planet. Your mentor would be the first to forbid it."

She lost a grip on her emotions in that moment and felt herself grimace. Some recollections resonated more loudly with her suppressed half, her mentor being one of them.

Arrogant, know-it-all ass.

Arrogant when it came to downplaying his own superiority but definitely knowledgeable—and unforgiving. "These are unusual circumstances. My mentor doesn't know the whole story. These people do not work for the *D'zpi.*"

"Yet they bear their slave technology. Our scanners detected the presence of their distinctive hardware embedded in the central cortex of the biological hosts."

"But they didn't have it placed there willingly. The cyborgs mean us no harm. They just want help and answers. They are not slaves to the *D'zpi*, or anyone else. They are free thinking, like me."

"Not entirely."

The *Zvali'dus* commander had a point. The cyborgs would never be completely untainted so long as the computer chip remained in their brain. Yet, removing it would probably kill them unless they could find nanobots willing to choose them.

"You can't sell them at auction. You know what type of beings will purchase them." Those who would hold the cyborg lives in small esteem. Expendable workers for dangerous mines, fodder for violent wars, playthings for perverse bordellos. "You'd be giving them unjust punishment for a crime they didn't commit."

"I am not interested in excuses for their existence, nor are we going to counter current standing orders. The abominations are not allowed near the source world." Even the *Zvali'dus* couldn't name it. "Their banishment is part of the *T'xa* charter we signed, and we are not about to compromise our agreement with them."

"I will not allow you to do this. I demand—"

She caught only a hiss of passing air before the tiny missile hit her.

Used to being invincible, Lilith was quite perturbed to find herself, for the second time that day, waking on a cot, but this time, in less desirable quarters.

They put me in a prison cell! One made for people like her. Forget traditional bars or holes in the ground. The more advanced species knew how to trap nanotech hosts. Pure power, disruptive and fatal to bots and flesh alike.

"Well, if it's isn't freaky girl. How nice of you to join us. Because it's so much nicer when I can ream an idiot out in person," Aramus grumbled, drawing her attention. "We can trust them, she says. They won't harm us." He squeaked the accusation in a high-pitched voice. "This is why I prefer to blow things up. At least then I get pretty lights and big explosions."

Despite the complaint, Lilith found herself glad to hear Aramus' voice. She'd, in a roundabout way, discovered her companions and no longer found herself alone. It meant it wasn't yet too late to save them. "I never said anything about trust. Never trust a slaver." Only the highest price brought their loyalty. "You should look on the positive side of our situation. They haven't harmed us. As far as I can see, your tongue is still functioning, and your cognitive ability to find fault with the situation is thriving."

Laughter, from more than one cyborg. "She's got your number, Aramus," Seth quipped.

"Fine. Laugh. That doesn't get us out of these cages. Got a bright idea for that, freaky girl?"

A valid question, but not the most pressing one for her. "Did everyone make it alive? Where is Avion?"

Anastasia pointed. "Down on the end. He's breathing, according to Seth, but he hasn't woken up yet."

"Are we all accounted for?"

"We are now that you've arrived, plus a few extra. You've never met them but say hello to the crew of the other explorer vessel in the cyborg fleet. Aphelion." A male a cell over waved. "Deidre, MJ, and Xylo." Faces that she matched to files she'd downloaded from the *SSBiteMe.* All cyborg and on a mission of exploration. A failed one obviously.

To better assess the situation, she required more information. "More cyborg prisoners? How did the *Zvali'dus* capture them?"

"Same way they got the *SSBiteMe.* They said halt or we'll shoot. Common sense made the decision easy."

"Lilith, have they said what they plan to do with us?" Anastasia asked from the energy-lined room beside her.

A telling frown creased her brow before she could stop it. Any time her emotions became intensely engaged, Lilith lost control of her body. Her stifled side grew stronger. Soon she might not be able to keep her locked away at all. "I know their intention. The *Zvali'dus* plan will not meet with your approval. Nor will it benefit Avion. They plan to auction you off at the nearest trader station or world."

"Sell this beautiful face? How brilliant. They'd make a fortune, which would probably make up for the loss they'd take with my best friend. For some reason, people think he's trouble."

"Don't you ever shut up?" Aramus growled.

Seth waggled his fingers at Anastasia and grinned. "Only when I'm kissing wifey poo."

"Or I gag him," she mumbled.

"Such sweet, sensual torture," Seth sighed.

"Um, guys, shouldn't we be planning our escape?"

"What do you think I've been doing? While we've been chatting, I've been multi tasking," Seth announced. "First, I save us from this prison."

"In other words, we're fucked." Aramus might lack elegance in his speech, but he knew how to get the point across.

"Aramus, really, why must you have so little faith?" Seth extolled as he stood in front of the force field. "Don't underestimate my desire to move on to Plan B and then C."

"What's Plan B?" Kentry asked.

"Take over this ship of course."

"And plan C?" Lilith asked, curiosity commandeering her tongue.

"Making sweet love to my wife."

"Which leads us back to our first problem. How do we get out of these cells?"

"I'll handle that part." Seth extended his hands to the energy wall.

"Seth. Don't touch it," Anastasia warned. "Remember what Aphelion said happened to Serge."

Lilith might not have been present, but she could imagine. Immediate vaporization. The intense concentration of pure electricity fried a person into the finest ash.

"I remember what he said, but I also don't want to stay in this cell. It's cramping my style, not to mention keeping me from you, wifey poo."

Lilith wasn't the only one who found herself watching in stunned silence as Seth's skin rippled. The flesh-like tone seemed to harden, the hue of it turning slightly orange. It took on a glossy sheen, a surreal one, as if his flesh had become something else entirely. He approached the energy wall.

"Seth!" Anastasia's voice rose into a screech as her husband stepped into the electrical field…and emerged on the other side.

More than one person gaped, Lilith included. "How did you do that?" she asked.

Obviously his skin change had something to do with it, but what had he done? Lilith had never thought to control her own body to the point that it changed physical properties. She would have said it was impossible. But then again, hadn't she gleaned over the years, as the military waged their war, that cyborgs exhibited a variety of abilities? More like impossible feats, or so her mentor had taught her.

Did he lie? Or are the cyborgs even more evolved than should be possible?

Seth certainly seemed to have a firm handle on his abilities. He brushed imaginary lint from his cream-colored shirt, more like flickers of electricity that sizzled and popped, not burning him. "You seem to forget sometimes our nanos are capable of so many miraculous things. Rapid repair. Harnessing ambient energy into a kinetic force. Surviving extreme temperatures. If it's capable of all those things, what about changing cellular structure? Becoming something new? In this case, a non-conducting material like plastic."

"You turned yourself into a freaking Ken doll?" Aramus seemed incredulous.

As for Lilith, she giggled. "Does that make Anastasia his Barbie?" Even she had cherished one of the buxom blonde dolls when the scientists and doctors were still in the early stages of testing. She'd loved her plastic friend.

She threw a pretty wild tantrum the day the psychiatrists took it away to see how she'd react.

It took them months to repair the damage, but the good news was they gave her a new doll. The doctor, however, who had the bright idea? He never came back.

The comparison of the dashing couple to the famous toys triggered mirth in all of them. Levity in the face of adversity. *I've done that, too, during some of my roughest moments.* Stress relief was okay, so Daddy said, but giggling while covered in blood surrounded by bodies, bad, very bad.

Aramus sobered first. "Now that we've finally gotten to confirm Seth's no better than a little girl's toy, it's time the rest of us escaped."

"I don't know if I'd suggest trying my method that quickly," Seth replied as he placed his palm on a console set in the center of the room adjacent to the hallway of cells. "It took me weeks to master it. I was looking for a way to counter Taser fire. Trust me when I say it's not as easy as it looks. Organic cells aren't too crazy about the whole switch to plastic."

"We can't stay in here," Aphelion said. "We're sitting tin cans."

"Which is why I'm poking the onboard computer. If you give me a minute or two, I'm currently working on hacking their system to free you all."

Time wasn't something they had an abundance of. Despite the lack of an audible alarm, Lilith suspected their captors knew of Seth's escape. While the *Zvali'dus* themselves might not prove formidable enemies, their guards were. The hulking lizard beings from a planet much like Earth in prehistoric times, the *daecrocs* would arrive armed and, at eight plus feet, capable of taking on the cyborgs.

Should I tell them? Avion seemed to think she needed to divulge more instead of waiting for direct questions, but her mentor told her to never tell what she knew. Everything was a secret. Except, Lilith had let some things slip.

Bad, bad girl. Master will punish us. An urge to hide almost had her running. Instead, she slammed a few doors shut on her other voice and shared her knowledge. "Once Seth deactivates the walls, we must hurry. The *daecrocs* will be coming."

"Would that be the giant dinosaurs that carted you in?" Xylo asked.

"Yes. They are extremely tough beings. Their skin is like an armor, very hard to penetrate. Their tails are barbed with a paralytic agent at the tips. They have only a few weak spots when it comes to hand-to-hand combat, like their eyes, of which they only have a pair in their head. They also have a version of an arterial vein in their necks, one on either side where the jaw connects."

"What about their hearts? Same spot as us?"

She shook her head. "Lower, and protected not just by their shell-like skin but a cage of bone. As I said, very hard to kill."

"About fucking time we ran into some decent competition," Aramus said as he cracked his knuckles. "Do you think they'll send enough for all of us to play with?"

She lost a hold on her jaw in that moment. *I think he might be crazier than me.* She almost clapped her hands in glee.

"There will be plenty of them to fight, and share"—*what a novel concept*—"if we are to take over this ship."

"Fighting. Hostile takeover. This plan is sounding better and better all the time," Aramus enthused. "Maybe you aren't so bad after all, freaky girl."

The backhanded compliment warmed her. Was the heat in her cheeks indicative of a blush? "In order to commandeer the vessel properly, we should hit a few key locations."

"Shh. Don't say them aloud," Seth said. "The surveillance cameras are still on. No need to tell them where we're going. Hold off until I get this blasted machine to behave."

"Don't force it, dude, stroke it," Kentry hollered. "Isn't that what you always say?"

Seth kept typing one-handed as his other hand raised and flicked a single digit.

Giggle.

"While we're waiting for the geezer spy model over there to get things done, what can you tell us about this ship?" Adam asked.

"This is a standard ark vessel. It is immense, dozens of decks, a few square miles in size. It can house thousands of beings."

"It's a fucking space city," Xylo exclaimed.

"Not quite," she corrected. "The vessel itself is not overly populated. The majority of the space is designated for cargo, organic cargo, although the *Zvali'dus* are open to carrying other goods. Most call them slavers since that is what they specialize in. However, they will trade anything that will turn a profit."

"We were caught by merchants." Aramus groaned. "The shame of it."

"Actually, their activities are more in line with the Earth definition of pirating."

"Really? We were captured by scurvy pirates? Epic." Aphelion wasn't the only one beaming at the news.

"How big of a crew are we talking about on board?" Aramus asked.

"The *Zvali'dus* tend to rely on their impressive outer defenses rather than internal ones, so they don't carry as many guards as they could." The reason being escapes just didn't usually happen. The cages were supposed to be foolproof. It would gall the slavers to know abominations had bested their system. "But we will encounter resistance, so arm yourself if you can."

"I got all the weapon I need." Aramus let a fearsome smile stretch his lips as he cracked his knuckles.

Old-school violence. Giggle. What fun.

"Okay, guys and girls, cameras are gone. Power bars coming down in twenty-eight seconds," Seth announced as he tapped at a blurring speed.

Aramus whistled and drew everyone's attention. "Now that the eyes in the walls are gone, listen up. Here's what we're going to do. Everyone snag a buddy as soon as the bars come down. Riley, you're with me."

"I've got wifey poo," Seth sang out.

"Doc's got my ass," Adam announced.

Everyone claimed a partner, even Lilith, whose claim of, "Avion is mine," didn't go unchallenged.

Avion is mine. How nice that sounded. Possessive too.

"Um, I hate to question you, Lilith. But how are you planning on lugging Avion? No offense, but the guy weighs a ton and you're not exactly on the robust looking side." Kentry questioned her ability to carry Avion to safety.

Laughter bubbled. "I could carry a pair of him and not tax myself. Do not judge me by my exterior. My nanos will play with the gravity around him in order to lessen his weight."

"Oh man, you have got to teach me that trick," Seth replied. "It would come in handy when wifey poo takes me shopping."

"She can teach you later. Right now we've got other shit to worry about. Now that we've got groups, Lilith, where are we going?" Aramus brought them back on track.

"Kitchens and the command center."

"Kitchen? I'm pretty sure no one needs to stop and have a snack during a violent uprising."

"Not the prisoners' kitchen. The guard one. More specifically, the livestock pantry. Threaten the guards' food source and you'll see the *Zvali'dus* lose control of the *daecrocs*. The lizards might work for money, but they live for fresh food."

"Are you fucking kidding me?"

She shook her head. "It is a strange weakness of theirs."

"If you say so," Aramus said with a skeptical note. "Aphelion, take your partner, MJ, along with Deidra and Xylo, Adam and Laura, Kentry and Rosalind to the kitchens. Kill whatever you have to but secure that area. The rest of us will follow freaky girl here to the command center."

"Aye, commander."

Everyone tensed in their cells as they waited.

"Three. Two, one." Seth counted down, and at zero, the bars on the prison rooms winked out. In scant seconds, they all vacated their cells, not wasting time as they met their partner and took off running. Or, in Riley's case, she ended up over Aramus' shoulder. The poor thing still suffered from a case of humanity.

A cure would have to wait for later. They needed to get moving.

The plan? Evade capture and attempt to take over the ship.

With that goal in mind, Lilith carefully grabbed Avion.

Seth and the rest clustered around her. "Wifey poo and I will take point. Aramus, you and Riley cover the rear. Lilith, you and Avion take the middle and give us directions to where we're going."

Help? How novel. *Remember your manners,* her inner voice chided. "Thank you." The not oft said words felt odd, but at the same time, having people around her who didn't try to drug her or keep her prisoner in general felt good.

"Don't thank me. This is what friends do. We cover each other's ass in battle."

Friendship at last?

Friends didn't let friends get shot, or so she could practically hear Avion saying, which was why, as they jogged the long and wide halls leading to the command deck, she projected a small force field in front of them to deflect the worst of the laser blast aimed their way by the soldiers they encountered.

After their sixteenth hard-earned kill, a slightly disheveled Seth observed, "I thought you said they didn't have much crew aboard."

"They don't. A true war vessel has thousands while we must deal with only a few hundred."

"A few hundred she says. Decent odds I'd say. Or is the old spy 'borg in need of a nap?" Aramus teased.

"You've been chatting with Adam, haven't you?" Seth grumbled right after he killed a gray-skinned being who thought the puny blaster he aimed at them would actually hold them at bay.

"I rather like the guy. He knows how to blow shit up."

"Your obsession with explosions is a tad disconcerting," Riley observed from her upside-down position. An armed position as Seth gave her the acquired blaster.

"You'd think you'd be used to explosions by now. You spend an awful lot of time together in his room." Seth winked, and Lilith couldn't understand why Aramus' coloring turned a bright shade of red.

Was the cyborg ill?

No, just angry. Again.

"At least my woman doesn't threaten to kill me."

Aramus dropped Riley and bellowed as he rushed a hulking lizard man who emerged from a T-intersection in the hall.

"Ah man," Seth sulked. "That will even up the kill numbers again."

"Poor baby. We'll just have to find you some more of these crocs to kill." Anastasia yanked the knife she'd acquired along the way from the side of the dead creature's neck. She ran her fingers over its bare arm. "Smoother than you'd expect. I really like the leather on this one. Do you think their skin would make a decent pair of boots?"

Lilith absorbed the banter. While not directly involved, she quite enjoyed the minor skirmishes, and best of all, Avion woke.

"What did I miss?" he asked, his tone somewhat groggy.

"We were jailed. But Seth turned into a giant doll and we escaped. We are now fighting reptiles on our way to take over the ship."

Avion groaned.

"Are you all right? Does something hurt?" she asked, flooded with concern for his wellbeing.

"Just annoyed I slept through all the action again. I really miss being a cyborg. I'm missing out on all the fun."

"Fun?" She said it questioningly because she could practically hear Daddy's voice, *"War isn't fun, but necessary."* However, in this case, given the natural adrenaline running through her body, her general level of contentment, not fabricated by a regulated release of the proper hormones to maintain a balanced physique, yes, she was having fun. Real fun. With friends.

Teehee. Look at me. And Daddy said I could never live in normal society.

Then again, not much about the cyborgs or this

situation was normal. There wasn't a set of rules or a handbook on how to act. A human one at any rate. She knew what her old mentor would say.

A host of the nanotech should always comport herself in a respectful manner. An old teaching that she'd pretty much forgotten. But, then again, a lot of what her mentor imprinted her with had been overwritten by the forceful will of her father.

Daddy Dear who locked me up and took away everything. Even her few friends among the staff.

However, now she had new friends, and they were depending on her.

She tossed up a shield, just in time, as a trio of *daecrocs* pounded into view. Then another trio.

"Finally a decent challenge," Aramus enthused.

"Big one's mine," Seth hollered.

"Too late." Anastasia smirked as she whirled, her blade having already sliced through a fatal vein.

"No fair."

"I called it."

"Too slow," Anastasia teased as she slid along the floor and sliced the inside of the *daecroc's* thighs.

A weak spot Lilith never thought to mention. Most beings wouldn't be crazy enough to try that maneuver. It seemed she'd not given the cyborgs enough credit when it came to fighting. She'd only ever observed the human recruits spar. Puny, quickly tired things that lacked grace and strength.

The cyborgs, however, were another thing entirely. Graceful. Violent. Efficient.

It was beautiful to watch.

But someone chafed at not being able to participate. Avion struggled in her arms. "Put me down."

"I can carry you. It does not tax me."

"Maybe, but it irritates the hell out of me. I'm not dead yet, and I'll be damned if I'll let my woman carry me around like a sack of bolts."

It occurred to Lilith that she was stronger and could ignore his request, but her other half prevailed. *A man has his pride. Let him keep it.* Besides, he'd called her his woman. She rather liked that designation.

On his feet, Avion shuffled until his fingers touched the wall.

"Woo. Last kill." Seth raised both hands in the air and did a triumphant strut.

"Show off," Aramus muttered.

Avion turned his head to face her, even though he couldn't see. She wondered how he always knew where she was.

"How much farther to our destination?" he asked.

"One last corner and then we'll have to tear our way through the riot shield door."

"What are the chances the hall is empty?" Seth asked.

"I'd say there is a zero percent probability. We will encounter resistance."

"Last kill gets to fly this thing," Seth whooped before sprinting around the corner.

He wasn't alone. Anastasia, Adam, and Aramus were at his heels. Riley tucked closer to Lilith and Avion, the gun in her hand steady, but, given her human status, probably not too accurate. Lilith would have to keep an eye on her, lest the female miss.

Violence erupted out of sight, but the aftermath lingered. Bodies littered the floor, and blood made the smooth floors slick.

Lilith kept watch on Avion as he walked with too much nonchalance through the battle zone. Blinded or not, Avion didn't seem to have too much difficulty navigating the littered hall. Even with his nanos gone, he was much more than a human.

However, he was fading. She needed to gain control of this ship and get them to where they needed to be.

The portal to the command area was sealed shut.

"Don't touch it," she warned as Seth neared it. "It's electrified."

Seth stopped a few feet short and stared at it. "How do we open it? I didn't think to bring a blowtorch."

"I usually do," Aramus grumbled. "It's in my kit bag on the *SSBiteMe*."

"Lilith, any ideas?" Anastasia asked.

"Yes. We wait."

"Wait for what? An invitation in?" Aramus snorted.

"Actually. Yes. If your other team is successful then…" *Hiss. Click.* The sealed door opened, and a squad of *daecrocs* with glaring yellow eyes and snarling teeth met them, weapons raised.

"Don't fire," Lilith ordered. "They're surrendering."

"That doesn't look like surrender to me," Aramus growled.

"Watch," Lilith said. She moved to stand in front of them all, confronting the towering creatures. She stared them in their baleful eyes and stated, "Our people have conquered the kitchens. We control the food supply. Drop the guns, or I will give the order to have the live cargo sucked into space."

"You think threatening to flush their fresh—" Aramus' rejoinder faded as the weapons pointed at their face dropped and hit the floor with a clatter. "Are you fucking kidding me? They're surrendering because we threatened to flush their steak?"

"Everyone has their price," Anastasia replied. "What's yours?"

The minute flick of Aramus' eyes toward Riley was telling. Lilith could also understand it. Some things were worth more than loyalty.

"The ship is ours," Lilith announced.

"You can't do this," the *Zvali'dus* slaver sputtered as he rose from his command seat. "This goes against the treaty."

"So does locking me up and threatening to sell my friends."

"Chosen ones do not behave in this fashion."

"Nor do they do this." Lilith leaned forward and licked the gray slaver, a big wet swab of tongue across his paper-dry cheek.

He squeaked. His eyes grew wide. He dared to slap her.

As if his puny blow could budge her. A smile on her lips—*nothing tastes sweeter than revenge*—she bent over and plucked a gun from the floor. In a single smooth motion, she straightened and aimed it at the slaver.

"You wouldn't dare," he sputtered.

She fired, and he hit the floor, the neat hole in his head nothing that could be repaired.

"What did you do that for?" Aramus barked.

Had Aramus forgotten? "Last kill gets to pilot the ship. Seth set the rules to the game. And I won."

Her victory went unchallenged, and she set the course to the planet that had made her who she was.

In a sense, I'm going home. But she wasn't counting on a warm welcome.

CHAPTER FIFTEEN

It chafed Avion that he couldn't play with his buddies or impress his girl with his skill. From the sounds of it, these *daecroc* things were the bomb to fight. *I so would have kicked some reptile ass.*

If he weren't broken. At least their escape and take over had gone according to plan.

If too easy.

The *daecrocs* escorted the remaining slavers to the prison cells and then withdrew to their ship, a massive vessel parked in a hangar bay. Once they loaded it with livestock, which Seth declared "the ugliest, hairiest smelliest beasts evah!" the lizard men departed.

Aramus didn't like it. "Damn it, and here I was looking forward to sparring with some of them later."

"Maybe we should have kept a few to play with."

"Boys and their pet lizards," Anastasia teased.

"I, for one, am glad they're gone," Riley announced. "They didn't smell too good."

Only Avion asked, "How come they're abandoning ship so easily?"

Lilith answered. "We've taken over the ship and imprisoned their employer. The *daecroc* don't owe them allegiance. Now that we've cut their source of revenue, why would they stay? They will simply hire themselves out to another crew."

As a matter of fact, the leader of the crocodile beings told Aramus to call if they ever had enough funds and needed help going to war.

As if the cyborgs would share that kind of glory.

The takeover went way too smoothly, and Avion didn't trust it, but then again, that might have had to do with the fact that distrust was easier to bear than hope.

Lilith seemed convinced this secret place they were going to held the answer to fixing him. Yet, from what he gleaned, the *Zvali'dus* seemed unwavering in their belief that all the cyborgs would be met with extreme prejudice.

Abominations.

They've even got a name for us. Avion couldn't help but be annoyed by the whole situation. *We don't fit on Earth. We can't escape in space. And, now, even the place that is the true origin of our nanotech affliction denies us.*

Where did they belong?

Where did he belong?

Avion couldn't claim a foot in any camp anymore, not cyborg or human. He was other. A dying, one-of-a-kind breed.

Yet Lilith didn't care. She didn't care if he was damaged. Broken. She wasn't with him because she admired his skill in battle or how he flew a ship. She just plain liked him.

She's nuts.

But with good reason, given her past. A past Avion didn't care about. He looked beyond her killer nature and otherness. To him she was Lilith, lovely, sweet, naïve and, at the same time, too wise.

It wasn't her fault she had issues. Lilith had many gaps in her memories, fractured recollections tainted by the young and still unschooled mind of a child.

He could see the battle in her as two sides of an opposing personality fought to share one space. How he wished he had the time to help her merge the two facets and accept herself for who she was, organic and tech.

Don't give up yet.

He couldn't have said if it was his voice or hers that told him that.

Once Lilith set the course, which the *Zvali'dus*

had programmed in their database, Lilith relinquished control of the ship to Aramus.

"That was nice of you," Avion said as she led him away, her hand tucked in his.

"I don't know if his mate would agree. Aramus was rubbing parts of the command center and calling it his precious and his sweet baby."

"Some people get off on collecting books or glass figurines. I love airplanes. But Aramus is a spaceship whore. The good news is Riley doesn't seem to mind."

"Part of that whole love thing again?" Lilith inquired.

"Now you're starting to get it."

"I believe I'm beginning to grasp it, but I'm still not sure I'm capable of feeling it."

Not seeing Lilith didn't mean Avion couldn't manage to manhandle her against a wall, his face inches from hers, his body pressed against hers. "You feel, Lilith. You might not always mean to, but a part of you feels emotions."

"I am not supposed to though. I was taught that emotions lack logic. That the right decisions come from analysis and forethought."

"And yet pleasure comes from letting go," he whispered against her lips, not quite touching her, but it didn't matter. She still shivered as his warm breath caressed her lips. "Let it all go, Lilith. I know you're keeping a part of yourself closed off."

"But if I let go, if I let the other half of me loose, what if I can never reel her back?"

By her, he understood she meant the human side she'd suppressed for so long, the slightly crazy part of her that chafed at its confinement. "Why would you want to box yourself away? You are more than just logic and nanotech. You are also human. A woman. A person with emotions and choice and depth. Who says all those sides can't cohabit together? It's what we cyborgs have achieved. And while I can't deny we're a little insane, who cares? Individuality is beautiful." *You are beautiful.*

She sighed against him. "I am tired of fighting her."

"Then don't. Set yourself free, vixen."

He pressed his lips against hers, their soft plushness a sensory delight even in his weakened state. She returned his embrace, opening her mouth for him and daring to let her tongue be the first to stray.

He sucked it. She made a sound of pleasure.

"A room?" he questioned. *I don't wish us to be disturbed for what I have planned.*

You should preserve your strength.

Fuck that. I need a reason to live, and that reason is you.

She almost crushed him as her arms came around his ribs and squeezed. It gladdened him that his words struck a chord with her, yet at the same time, it saddened him. One, because it was so obvious she was starved for affection. And, two, despite her belief, Avion couldn't promise he'd stick around to give her the love she so ardently deserved.

But altruism was for someone else.

Avion was selfish. Dying or not, he needed to taste her one last time. Needed to show her that she was a woman, not just a host governed by the machines that existed within her. A woman with needs and emotions.

A woman with desires…

The room they stumbled into didn't have a bed, but it did have a door that locked and a couch, or so she announced before she pushed him down on it. He might have protested her take-charge attitude, but he allowed it since she followed him, straddling his waist, the gown she wore riding up her thighs.

Without his eyes to show him, he relied entirely

on his sense of touch. He reveled in the silky softness of her skin as his fingers trailed across her thighs and over the swell of her hips to rest on the indent of her waist.

The rustle of fabric teased him. "What are you doing?" he asked.

"Removing my clothes."

"You are nude?"

She grabbed his hands and placed them upon her perky breasts. His hands cupped them, thumbs brushing across already erect peaks. "Entirely nude. But you are not. Yet."

Her smaller yet deft hands divested him of his shirt, baring his torso to the satiny fabric of the couch. He lifted his hips for her as she yanked at his loosely fitted trousers. At her gasp, he could so easily imagine his cock springing forth, thick and hard. He didn't need eyes to know she stared at it, but her sudden touching of his shaft drew forth a groan from him.

"You like it when I touch you?"

"Love it. Just like I love touching you. Feeling you." He let his fingers roam her skin, tracing her every curve, feeling her every shudder. She couldn't hide the smell of her arousal, the musky perfume mouthwatering. The moistness of her core wetted his lap where she sat straddling him.

But he wanted more than her to touch him. He craved a taste.

Gripping her around the waist, he tugged.

"What do you try to do?" she asked.

"I want to lick you."

"Lick me where?"

Instead of saying it aloud, he let a single finger stroke across her damp folds.

She shuddered. "Oh. *Oh.*"

Lucky him, she didn't have further questions, merely compliance to his wish. With his head leaned back, he felt rather than saw as she brought her sex to his mouth. He nuzzled her mound, the soft down of her pubes tickling. He kissed his way down to his goal, and she shuddered in his grip.

Despite her squirming, he held her as firmly as he could, his hands anchored to her hips as he brought his lips to her sex and flicked her with his tongue.

A low moan emerged from her.

He licked again, a long, wet swipe then a short one. He lapped at her moist core, spreading her nether lips and tasting her sweet honey. Slender fingers threaded through his hair and tugged, pulling at him almost painfully, but he welcomed it. It kept him focused and aware that, for as much pleasure as he got from this, hers was tenfold.

As if they had all the time in the world, he let his tongue and mouth explore the sweetness of her sex. He located her clitoris, a swollen nub, which, when nibbled on, had her hips bucking and her sex thrusting at his face.

Awash with pleasure, Lilith allowed herself to feel and not control. She let loose, and he reveled in it. He also wanted more.

More of her.

As his tongue lightly flicked her pleasure button, he inserted one then two fingers within her channel. Her muscles squeezed around him, wetly pulsing. He thrust them in and out as his tongue teased her. He pumped and licked and panted as he felt her pleasure tightening, evident in the tension humming through her body.

She pushed on his fingers, trying to drive them deeper, but they didn't have the length she craved.

Only one thing did.

"I want," she gasped.

"I know what you want," he growled. He placed one last kiss on her sex before pushing at her hips, drawing her down.

She grasped his intent and guided her body the rest of the way. The head of his cock hit the opening to her core, and then he was sheathed.

His turn to have his hips buck and for him to cry out. She took him. All of him. Deep and tight.

Astride his lap, Lilith rocked back and forth on his shaft, driving him in and squeezing him so perfectly. Panting hard now, he did his best to keep up, but Lilith was the one in control now. With her hands splayed across his chest, she rode him, fast and hard. She rose and dropped on his cock with force. She squirmed on his lap, pushing him deep.

He couldn't hold on. It was too much. Not enough. Too good. Too…

"Lilith!" He yelled her name as he came, and she said his too, but in his mind.

Avion. Her affection for him surrounded him, along with the blissful glory of their orgasm, a meld of spirit, body, and mind that had him wrapping his arms tight around her, determined to never let her go.

Until death do us part.

Which, unfortunately for him, came too fast.

CHAPTER SIXTEEN

Finally she understood the expression, *I wish this moment could last forever.*

Some pleasures you never wanted to end. Unfortunately reality stopped for no one, not even a chosen one.

Lilith disengaged herself from Avion, who'd fallen asleep.

Did we kill him?

A slight panic infused her as she checked him over. A sigh left her. No, he wasn't dead. He rested, exhausted by the exertion, even if he insisted on it, too much for his taxed system. Yet, Lilith couldn't say no. She knew Avion recognized his approaching mortality, and much as she tried to deny it, she saw it too.

However that doesn't mean I'm not going to fight for him to live with everything I've got.

And everything she had was on a planet she couldn't even name aloud and a person she could only recall as her mentor.

No face. No name. Nothing but a subtle remembrance of his voice and his teachings. *Don't allow the emotional side of your host control you. The nanotechs know what is right. The bots will show you the correct path.*

But the correct path for who?

A return to the bridge showed Aramus sharing the command seat with Riley, who sat tucked in his lap, napping. Kentry manned a console along with Rosalind, a fierce Latina with distinctive machine orb eyes. Her otherness would not be well received.

It might be best if she's not one of the first to meet my mentor.

He'd take one look at her cyborg additions and order her destruction. Actually, he'd probably instantly spot all the cyborgs as impure ones, despite their normal appearance.

I need to talk to him first. Explain what happened.

Surely when he found out the depravity the cyborgs had suffered he'd understand.

A futile hope. She knew too well from her time with humans that logic often lost to fear—and in the case of her mentor, tradition.

Their run of good luck ended when they hit the airspace outside their target planet. Control of the vessel was wrested from Aramus, despite his colorful cursing.

"What the fuck is happening?" he bellowed.

"We are in their airspace now. They have a satellite system capable of generating a pulse that knocks the navigational systems of encroaching ships offline."

"That's not good."

"It's normal."

Also normal was getting towed in to the planetary spaceport, as were the massive robotic guards who manned the gangplank when Lilith presented herself. Not alone. Aramus refused.

"I like you, freaky girl, but we haven't known each other long, so how do I know it's not a trap?"

He raised a valid point. Trust was earned.

Given her mentor's attitude, Lilith took Seth and Anastasia with her. Laura and Adam too. Nothing in their outward appearance would announce their cyborgness, but her mentor would know. His nanotech would tell him.

As Lilith descended the ramp, bright lavender-hued sunlight made her blink. She'd forgotten the intensity of the planet's suns, a pair of them that kept this world well lit and, yet, not overly warm.

For a moment, as she basked in true daylight, the

first in years, she forgot why she was here and what she was about to do. She lifted her face and let the rays dance along her skin. She absorbed the ultraviolet, breathed in the fresh air tinged with a hint of floral. The planet—*E'dann, it's called E'dann*—truly was a paradise world. Lush with foliage. The water proved abundant and fresh. The fruits of the trees and bushes sweet and juicy. The inhabitants, non-lethal and tasty when roasted over a fire pit. How her mentor freaked the day he caught her human group out hunting then eating the product of their labor.

Nanos don't need to ingest the flesh of beasts. We can absorb whatever nutrients we need from the air, water, and ground. He preached it. He made them eat it. But it didn't mean the humans ever lost their craving for food. Real food.

"You were not supposed to return."

The bold statement shook her free from the memories. How had she gotten so distracted? Usually her nanos kept her mind on a more productive track. Lilith glanced toward the speaker. Tall and humanoid in shape, he wore an unadorned crimson cloak, the cowl draping his head and placing his face in shadow. He didn't need any badges or marks to announce who he was. Everyone knew.

Master Z'. Her mentor. A male, very much like a human man, who didn't seem as tall as she recalled but was definitely just as overbearing.

She executed a short bow. "Master Z', it has been some time since we last saw each other."

"Not long enough. You were not supposed to return, and you most especially should have never come dragging abominations with you."

"She didn't drag us, if it makes a difference. We came willingly." Seth had stepped forward to flank her in a show of support. "We found this lovely lady languishing in a cell and set her free."

"The humans imprisoned you?" Even though he said it as a query, Master Z' showed no other emotion.

"Yes, for a long time, that is when they weren't experimenting." *Needles. Blood. Skin scrapes. Lab tests. No better than a rat.*

"What of the other chosen ones? Are they prisoners too?"

"At first. Then the military killed them. All of them not long after our return. Only I am left."

"Barbarians," her mentor muttered. "Unworthy of the tech."

"Not all of them are like that."

"Enough to prove further selections from Earth are not worth the effort."

"I wouldn't say that. I've met many fine people." She gestured to Seth and the others. "My friends aren't like the ones who imprisoned me and killed the others."

"No, they're not. They're worse. They are infected. Impure. They offend me, and I refuse to discourse with you in their presence."

Said in a perfectly modulated tone, and yet, was it only Lilith or did it still sound petulant?

"Now hold on just a second there, buddy," Adam stepped forward, but Laura held him back.

"You do realize those robot guards of his outnumber us," Laura hissed.

Adam flicked a gaze to his left and right. "So?"

"So, it means we have to show diplomacy," Seth said on a sigh. "We're here to ask for help for Avion, and breaking all these wind-up toys probably won't work to our advantage."

Lilith bit the inside of her cheek, lest she giggle. Master Z' wouldn't understand her mirth just as she feared he wouldn't understand why the cyborgs were different.

I'll have to show him somehow.

"May I speak with my mentor alone?" she asked her friends.

"Are you sure?" Seth's glance behind her implied a concern about her safety.

"I'm sure. He won't harm me." She hoped.

Once her companions returned to the ship, her mentor spun on his heel and strode away, his booted feet marking a smooth cadence on the perfectly aligned stone pathways. Everything around them was meticulously arranged, from the cobbled paths and cut stone to the identical block buildings made to efficiently house the robots and all their supplies.

Master Z' liked order. *Or is it the nanotech that demands it of him?*

She'd never thought to wonder before. He kept walking, and she skipped to catch him.

"I need your help."

"I sense nothing wrong with your host body or nanotech. Although I have to wonder if your programming has somehow been corrupted."

The insult might have stung her younger self, but she'd suffered much worse than a verbal barb since she'd left E'dann. "The help isn't for me, but Avion, a male on board the ship."

"Another abomination?"

Had she sounded so disparaging when she used the same word? "Yes. And no. His bots are dead."

"Then he is not a chosen one."

"But he could be."

"Doubtful."

Said without even meeting him. She bit her tongue in an effort to control it. Her other side had some choice words to spew to her judgmental mentor, none of them polite or likely to advance her cause. "Even if he's not, you could help him. He needs healing."

No hesitation. "No."

"Please. He'll die if you don't."

"Doesn't matter. I still won't heal him."

"Why not?" Lilith stared at Z' trying to comprehend, but she couldn't fathom a valid reason for his refusal.

Z' could help. He had the knowledge, skills, and tools to do so. Access to science and medicine that didn't rely on the nanos. He had it and yet deliberately chose to withhold it.

That made her very angry. *Let's rip his eyes out. Punch a hole through his stomach. Stomp on his face.* She dug nails into her palms, a physical reminder to keep them by her side. Violence wouldn't help in this instance. Barely, she held on to the reins of her temper. For now.

"You actually have to ask why?" Master Z' spun to face her, and she finally caught a glimpse of his eyes, where a galactic storm brewed in a craggy face that while young in many senses—wrinkle-free, smooth bronzed skin, a full head of dark hair, a straight nose, and square jaw, not exactly a handsome man, but certainly arresting—was immovable in his beliefs. "He is an abomination. They all are. You know the nanotech was not meant to be enslaved in such a fashion, and yet you dare return bringing these *things* in tow. You! A creator of these impure beings. You are a disgrace. You ignored everything I taught you."

"I didn't have a choice. They enslaved me. Hurt me. Did things to curtail my power."

"You surely had options."

"You mean dying? I didn't realize being a host required I make a martyr of myself. And it's not something my nanotech ever suggested."

"Apparently your nanotech weighed the situation and thought there was still a chance for redemption. Which should have occurred when you did escape with these things. You had an entire journey where you could have rectified the wrong."

"Rectified? What are you saying?"

"You did not exterminate the impure ones when you should have. Nay, instead, you precipitated violence against our allies and brought with you the objects of your travesty."

When he put it that way, he made it sound kind of bad. Except for one thing. "Stop blaming me. This is not my fault. I didn't make them. The human military did. I wasn't given a choice. Nor were they. For years they were slaves, but then something happened. They found their humanity. They think for themselves. Did you not see them? Even with the *D'zpi* chip, they are their own masters. They are not controlled."

Master Z' let out a snort, the disparaging sound so surprising she almost stumbled.

"So just because these abominations are reportedly sentient, that is supposed to make up for the nanos that are compelled in their blood?"

"So they're not perfect."

"An understatement. And you want me to fix one of them? To aid the slave host in keeping the nanotech prisoner?"

"Avion, the man who needs healing, doesn't have live nanos. The military found a way to kill them. It's why I came here."

He didn't seem surprised, judging by his answer. "It is because his neural interface threw the kill switch."

"Their brain chips have that ability?"

"All chipped machines do. It is the *D'zpi* protection against the enslaved tech taking over all organic life."

"If you know of that switch, then you can fix it. Turn it back on so his bots reanimate and heal him." Simple. Flick it, and poof, Avion would heal.

His next words sank her hope. "The switch

works only one way. Dead bots can't come back to life."

"I refuse to believe that. There must be a way."

"Sure there is, but I wouldn't recommend it."

"Tell me."

"It involves removing all the foreign parts in him, flushing his body of the blood and all the dead bots, and then introducing him to the pool to see if some of the tech will accept him as a host. However, that won't happen."

"Why not?"

"Because I won't allow it. This is not how things are done. Candidates for the tech are carefully chosen. They must adhere to the criteria set forth."

"You didn't care about that criteria when you placed me in the program."

"You were an exception."

"You were bribed to take me." She didn't recall specifics, but her father had leaked enough for her to glean that, in exchange for taking Lilith and attempting to heal her, Z's people would be allowed to take some Earth resources like water, lumber, and all the humans they wanted.

"A business transaction that worked in all our favors."

A little girl in exchange for goods. And Master Z' thought the cyborgs were an abomination? She really had to wonder. "So do me a favor now."

"You have nothing to offer. By your own words, your people have rejected you, which means you cannot make a treaty. You've broken numerous of our rules, and now you would ask me to break more? Why should I go against our beliefs?"

"Our beliefs? Or yours?"

"Does it matter? I see no reason to break tradition. No valid argument for your request."

"Because Avion will die if you don't." The very

thought filled her with a sucking sadness that dragged at her emotions.

"That makes no difference to me."

What a callous bastard. For once, her other voice said it perfectly. Z's refusal to listen made her scream, a wordless yell that finally startled a reaction from him.

"What are you doing?"

The last note of her cry still echoed before she replied. "I am expressing emotion. Something you, with all your teachings, don't seem to know anything about. Were you always this clinical?" Was her master always this cold and calculating? Good grief, was this how Lilith treated others, as if they were just objects, things of no worth or feelings?

It horrified her to realize that a part of her was just as cruel and uncaring as the supposed evolved being before her. All the enhancements in the world could not make someone grasp compassion.

This is what happens when you try to suppress your emotions. Her inner self, far from snide, said it rather sadly. For once, Lilith didn't immediately slam the door shut. For years, she'd tried to lock away that voice along with its emotional wisdom and ranting. Perhaps it was time she let the other half of herself have more of a say.

I don't want to be like Master Z' and view the world so strictly. Caring might prove tumultuous, but it sure beats the sterility of a life void of emotion.

"I am beginning to think that the nanotech severely erred when selecting you as a host. You have not adapted or followed our teachings well at all."

"That's because I am not a drone. Or a robot. Or a mindless being. I am Lilith." She straightened her spine and stared him straight in the eye. "I have feelings. Thoughts. And emotions. I do not wish to make choices based on logic. I want to be happy."

Z' actually snorted. "Happiness is overrated."

"But you know of it, or else you wouldn't claim that," she prodded.

Something flickered in his expression. A muscle might have tightened across his forehead. What past did Master Z' hide? "I once knew the wildness you speak of. Once upon a time, I, too, let feelings control me." For a moment sadness stormed across his eyes, a blue swirling agony that briefly touched her before his usual placid expression overtook it. "But I learned that happiness is fleeting. Uncontrollable. Only with logic can we truly live without chaos."

"What if I want the chaos?" she asked softly.

Again with the slight twitch in his face. "Why are you so determined to save this abomination? You have known him but a scant time. He is broken. Impure…"

"Kind. Gentle. Funny. But most of all, he sees me. Not as an object or a tool or a host for another life form. He sees me as a person." *And I'm pretty sure I love him.*

Her mentor had no reply initially. Z' spun from her and stared out the grand window spanning the chamber. The surreal view of the purple mountainsides, the striated rock peppered with brighter splashes of red as foliage struggled to grow was pretty. However Lilith couldn't appreciate the beauty, not when she was involved in a discussion that would decide the wellbeing of her friends—and maybe save Avion's life.

Z' continued to stare out the window even as he spoke in a low tone. "Once upon a time, in a past forgotten by everyone, I loved someone. A female, from the same planet as me. She was the sum of my world. On a mission of exploration, we came across a drifting ship unlike any we'd ever seen. Inside, there were no bodies. No pilot. Nothing. Just a pool of energy that beckoned.

"The nanotech?"

"Yes. A war had nearly wiped them out in a part

of the universe so far none have gone and ever returned. But I didn't know that then. All I knew was the pool called to me. They wanted me to touch it. So I did. I was chosen to become." His eyes rose to the sky, a supplicant to the recollection of a defining moment in his life.

"You became a host to the nanos and somehow became their guardian."

"I became. But my lover didn't."

"The nanos rejected her. And you did too?" Lilith didn't understand why he told her this. Lilith would never abandon Avion. She didn't care if he bore tech or not. She simply enjoyed his presence.

"I am not that shallow," he practically shouted the words in an outburst she'd never seen. "I still loved her. I begged my nanos to accept her, but she was part *D'zpi*. A very small part, but even then, they were enemies." He paused, and his shoulders hunched. "I did what I could with science and medicine, but in the end, as do all organic species, she aged and died. Without the nanotech, I could not keep her alive."

The ultimately sad love story. "So, you refuse to save him because he might die eventually?"

"I do this to save you the pain of losing him." He whirled on her, and his face was drawn into a rictus of agony. "You've known this male, what, a few days? He is still easily forgotten. You can still save yourself from the emotional crush that will overcome you when he dies. I do this now so you will not suffer later."

"But that's not your choice to make. I care for him. Killing him now or later, that won't change. All of us are mortal. Even you. You might have lived longer than most beings, but you can still be killed."

"I can't. I must protect the tech." Said so wearily.

"Did it ever occur to you to share the burden? That you've punished yourself over her death long enough?"

"Share?"

"Sharing is caring." She blurted the words without thought, and he whirled around to eye her.

"Sharing is caring?" he repeated, arching a brow.

She shrugged. "It's an Earth expression, and something the cyborgs believe in. They are incredibly resilient and honest. Their bond to one another is enviable. You and the tech might have saved my life a long time ago, but at the same time, you stole it. Like the military, you sought to impose your views and to make me someone I'm not. I'm not just a host. Not just a means of spreading the tech. I am Lilith, and I want things, even if some of them might make me sad. Or angry. But that choice should be mine. I deserve a chance to experience life to its fullest." *I deserve a chance at happiness.*

"He means that much to you?"

"He does. They all do." *They're my friends.* She could say it without a giggle.

The resigned expression on Z's face made her heart flutter.

"Because I am irrationally fond of you, which means I am probably due for a system check, I will allow you to attempt to save your friend. However, I warn you, there is a high probability he will die."

"He will die if we do nothing."

"Since you insist on this, have him brought to the building adjoining the temple. I'll have medical tools for the two doctors you have on board. We will need them to cut the hardware from his body if there is any chance this will work."

"Thank you." On impulse, she threw her arms around her mentor.

He stiffened, his thick body as yielding as a tree trunk. To her surprise, his arms came around her in an awkward hug.

"Don't thank me yet. This might not work."

But at least it was a chance.

A chance that others had plenty to say about.

"Are you nuts?" Laura exclaimed. "That microchip in his brain is embedded. If we remove it, we'll probably kill him."

"It's the only way," Lilith repeated. "We must purge his body of all non-organic parts, especially the *D'zpi* programmed ones, if we are to have a chance of making this work."

Riley shook her head. "It can't be done. I have to agree with Laura here. While we can get rid of his robo eyes easily enough, his mechanical heart, not to mention his skeletal structure, can't be removed. As for his BCI, we could slice it from him, but the damage it would cause might leave him a vegetable."

"That's mineral if you don't mind," Avion whispered, lucid for the moment, but oh so very weak.

Lilith squeezed his fingers. *I know it's a huge risk, but Z' is convinced the BCI is the problem. It has to come out, or else it will keep telling the bots to shut down.*

He caught her mental projection and replied aloud. "Let's do it. I've always been a risk taker. This is no different. I either die in this bed, without a fight, or I take a chance."

With Avion determined, it didn't take much organizing to get them to the temple where Z' waited.

He'd changed his crimson robe for one of pure white. The entire temple was a blinding ivory with marble buffed to a high gleam and pure metal accents highlighting their glare. As Lilith looked around at a place she'd only seen once before while still a little girl, she couldn't help but frown.

This was a church. An alien one, unlike any on Earth, but still it was a place of worship for a religion, one dedicated to the nanotech.

The pool, a large round basin in the room with beveled metal edges, extended down into the floor. Who knew how far. Staring into it hypnotized a person, all those dancing bright sparks of light. Motes of energy and…life?

On the far side of the pool, upon a dais several steps high, sat a throne. Master Z's seat of power.

She remembered seeing him seated there, head held regally high as he went through his precious ritual, and one by one, the supplicants were given the tech—and judged.

As part of the ritual, there was an altar. The carved stone bed resided at the foot of the pool. A potential host lay upon the surface, hands clasped, eyes closed. The nanos would then ride up the channel that led from the edge of the pool and flow over the altar. They *tasted* the applicant. If they liked what they found, then some stayed. If they didn't, back they flowed into the electrical pond.

There was one difference from her recollection though, such as a hovering trolley upon which there was an array of tools, tools Master Z' took exception to.

"You cannot operate on him here. The applicant must arrive free of the impurities."

"He needs to be here, next to the source. Any farther and he'll bleed out before we can douse him with bots." Laura planted her hands on her hips and actually tried to stare down Lilith's mentor.

She quite enjoyed it. "Laura is right. Since you insist we remove the hardware, and the process is so risky, we need proximity. You know it and so does your programming."

When ritual interfered, throw common sense at a rational being to fluster it.

Z' beetled his brows. "Exactly how many rules do you expect me to break?"

"As many as it takes for you to listen to reason," she snapped.

"If he doesn't want blood in his temple, then we'll do it in the hall," Avion said, awake for the moment but leaning heavily against the altar.

"You would desecrate this place with your dirty blood. Such barbarians." Z's disapproval rang through loud and clear.

"Oh for fuck's sake. This is getting stupid," Aramus grumbled. While quiet up until now, he finally snapped.

And did the one thing that left them all speechless. He grabbed Avion and tossed him in the nanotech pool.

CHAPTER SEVENTEEN

Imagine the worst pain then multiply it by infinity.

If Avion could have screamed, he might have. But he doubted he'd find the air to make a sound because even simple acts like breathing or having his blood circulate proved beyond him.

I think I'm dying.

Problem was it was taking its sweet fucking time.

And it hurt.

Did the pain mean he lived still? If he did, then where was he? What had happened?

He floated, not in water or air. The hum of a million itty-bitty particles kept him aloft, or did they drag him down? It was impossible for him to determine, his sense of orientation completely skewed.

Perhaps he should call for help. He opened his mouth to see if he could cry out, but the tingly particles poured in. The buzzing microscopic bits burrowed into every hole in his body. Mouth, ears, nose, his very pores. The humming hive of bots sifted through him, testing his biological components, zipping along neural pathways before reaching his brain.

And halting.

They probed the foreign object in it. They could see it was attuned to one who had left because it found a host. Yet the biological being they probed wasn't the host. He—yes, it was male—was free. Should they test him?

Indeed they should. They needed to spread, lest the enemy find them and eliminate. They swarmed the foreign object. Its signal bounced off them harmlessly, deadly only to the bots it was tuned to. But they didn't like this vile impurity.

They absorbed its components and expelled those they could not use. Without the fetters, the mind lay open to them.

Brains…

Much like zombies—*hey, didn't I watch a movie about them in my teens?*—the bots latched on to Avion's brain and siphoned. Not flesh, no, they were more assiduous than that. They went after his memories.

Like his recollection of…toast.

The perfect piece of course. Crisp and evenly browned, spread with peanut butter. The smooth, not crunchy kind, that would melt on the hot bread and coat his mouth in nutty goodness.

Until he was allergic and any kind of nut sent him into anaphylactic shock.

His mind flitted to something else. The thrill of riding his bike down a hill, pedaling as fast as he could, until his momentum grew too great. His feet lost their rhythm and slipped from the pedals. His hands gripped the handlebars tight, but still he wobbled and waggled. And when he hit the rock, he flew. *Look at me, I'm—* Ouch.

The buzz moved on to the next memory.

Faster and faster, the tech hummed and learned while he drifted alone. And sank. Sank.

Rejected. Too defective. Impure. Too emotional. Not worthy.

I'm sorry, Lilith. The nanotech had spoken. Avion would die. Die alone.

Oh no you're not.

Of a sudden, Avion stopped his descent in the vast pool of waiting bots. Invisible arms wrapped around him and hugged him tight.

I'm here, Lilith whispered to his mind. *Don't listen*

to these less-than-perfect alien beings. You are worthy. I see you. And you have meaning.

Around Avion, the buzz rose in pitch, a billion voices crying out, not understanding how one of their hosts could question their brilliance. How could she claim they were wrong?

Because you don't understand love.

Love, what did the firing of emotional synapses have to do with anything?

Let me show you. Lilith merged her mind with Avion, not in a takeover but more to show the two sides of the equation.

What is love?

Love was the first time you heard their voice and couldn't help but find yourself drawn, intrigued, eager to discover more.

Love was knowing you'd found someone to stand by your side, even in danger, someone who wouldn't let you down.

Love was a sizzling touch, an electrifying glance, a sensual kiss that ignited passion.

As an example, Lilith reran the memory of their first embrace for the nanotech. A cherished moment. How Avion had wanted to stay in that magical moment forever. The ardent awareness that arced between them. The heated arousal, which flushed them both. The general happiness at just being with her. Being with Lilith.

Even more amazing, with their minds linked, Avion saw the same wonder from her memories. How she reveled in his touch, his affection. She also cherished that first true lover's touch.

Avion forgot about why they delved into his memories. The only thing he truly cared about now was expressing them to the one person who mattered.

I love you, Lilith.

And I love you. All of me does.

Machine and biological.

The nanotech surrounding him almost went still as they tried to compute this most strange of things. Machine couldn't rely on emotion to make its choices. Emotions were chaos. They couldn't be depended on. Or could they?

Avion could practically hear the collective hives' thought process. Perhaps the nanotech needed to expand its knowledge. It seemed there were gaps that needed answers.

We need to know more.

But, in order to explore, the bots required an uncontaminated vessel.

Holy fuck that hurts.

Avion opened sightless eyes wide, his mouth gaped, his body arced, the force of his agony driving ghost Lilith from him.

The pain, which had receded in the background, returned with a flamboyant "Aha!" and it brought friends. Lots of them.

His mechanical heart pounded, faster and faster. Slower and slower. It stopped.

Oh shit.

How long until he died? How long until—

Thump.

The slight thud barely registered.

Thud. Thump.

It came again, a steady beat, which grew stronger and stronger as his new organ grew from the absorbed remains of his old one.

Nerve endings sizzled as the bots embedded themselves into the very cellular structure of his body. Piece by piece, they cleansed him of the impurities the military had embedded in him. Cell by cell, they took over his system and mended his damage.

His eyes tingled.

Tingled?

Lids, which he'd not realized he'd closed, opened, opened to a blinding white light that surrounded him.

I can see.

He could also breathe and move his limbs.

Even if the medium he hung in wasn't liquid, Avion still swam in it. With powerful strokes, more powerful than he ever recalled, he headed for the surface.

He broke the humming skin of the nanotech pool. The warm air in the chamber bathed his newborn skin, and he said newborn because every sensation upon it was absorbed as if new. Without his BCI, and flooded with new bots, every experience was renewed. Despite the nanotech's vast knowledge, some things would have to be relearned, such as the feel of air upon his face. But as they learned from his experiences, so he discovered from them, if he knew the right questions to ask.

With the nanos, you sometimes didn't realize the answer until you went intentionally looking for it, a strange symbiotic system, which he understood was created so as to not overwhelm the host.

So much to learn. Experience. Live for.

I'm alive. And he couldn't wait to see Lilith.

As had become the habit when Avion recovered his senses, Aramus was yelling at his vixen.

"What do you mean those fucking bots rejected him? Avion's one of the good guys. If anyone deserves another chance, it's him."

"I showed them that, but…" Her shoulders hunched.

None of them knew the bots had changed their mind.

"Aramus, leave my girlfriend alone before I kick

your ass." Avion didn't bother watching Aramus for his reaction, too intent on Lilith as she whirled and beheld him.

Shock widened her swirling eyes. "Avion! You live." A smile pulled her lips wide, a smile he reciprocated.

"Apparently, your argument worked. The bots seem to think they can learn something from me and decided to give me another chance."

At his reappearance and words, faces crowded around the pool, but none was so daunting as that of the massive male Lilith called Master Z'.

"They cleansed you of the impurities," he stated with tight lips.

"Yup. Apparently, I'm all flesh and blood now. Even my eyes." Which he used to wink at Lilith. She smiled, and her cheeks pinkened.

Z's brow wrinkled. "Impossible. Their very own rules state only the biologically pure will be chosen."

"Haven't you ever heard, big guy? Rules are made to be broken," Seth announced.

Someone didn't like that answer. Galactic storm clouds brewed in his eyes. "And violators of the sacred pool are to be arrested. You dare to break the sanctity of this place with your antics."

"So Avion went for a swim instead of getting doused. Who cares? The end result is your precious bots accepted him, and he's all better," Aramus argued.

"One does not go for a swim in the sacred pool of tech," Z' said through clenched teeth.

"Dude, you seriously need to chill. I mean, what's so special about a pool of nanobots? Looks refreshing if you ask me."

Before anyone could stop him, Seth hopped into the sizzling mass, alongside Avion. And promptly sank.

"Idiot," Z' exclaimed. "You do not understand.

The nanotech is not a toy to be played with."

"We understand that you are the cause for a lot of shit, mister. Because of you, all of us have been changed. We lost our birth families. Our homes. Our right to a peaceful existence. We are fugitives because of what you did to Lilith and the others." Deidre, who'd not said much until now, let forth a tirade.

Planting her hands on her hips, Anastasia also had a few choice words for him. "And I'll thank you to not call my husband an idiot. You don't know him well enough to be able to express just how dumb he is. Now if you'll excuse me, I'd better go grab him."

Avion snickered at the look on Z's face as she dove elegantly in.

"You are all barbarians."

"No, we're cyborgs, and don't you forget it, asshole."

"You don't know what you've done. The trouble your very presence causes."

"Lighten up." This from Kentry, who rolled his eyes for good measure. "You're acting like it's the end of the world."

Actually, it was, but no need to let the others know yet.

"Um, isn't anyone else worried about Seth and Ana?" Riley asked as she leaned over the edge and peered.

Avion cocked his head, listening as the hum answered her question. "They're both fine. Just getting some of their parts revoked for better ones."

"You mean they're getting rid of the metal?" Aramus blinked.

"Every last bit. It seems the tech is eager for some new hosts. As a matter of fact, it suggests you all jump in."

"No. You can't—" Z' actually seemed at a loss,

as almost everyone present hopped in except for Riley, the one last true human, and Lilith. Even Laura, who held a pure form of the tech, joined the party, laughing as she stroked after Adam.

Watching them, Riley bit her lip.

"Why do you not join the others?" Lilith asked. "The tech will not hurt you."

"It's not me I'm worried about," she mumbled as she cupped her belly. "But the baby."

Aramus' head broke the surface just as she said that, and his bellow of, "What baby?" could probably be heard for galaxies around.

"The one you impregnated me with, idiot. It seems your assumption that you're all sterile might have been a tad premature. Apparently, you're not so much sterile as your bots are providing birth control. Or, in our case, removing it."

"You're pregnant." Saying it aloud, Aramus sounded almost terrified.

"Congrats, old pal," Avion said and then saved his friend by shoving his head back under. The bots weren't done with him yet, and Riley didn't need to see the process involved when a man with a literal metal plate in his head had it absorbed and a skull reconstructed.

Since he didn't need to be in the pool anymore, which was now getting crowded, Avion placed his hands on the side and vaulted free.

How he loved the return of his strength and vitality. *I can see.* See his vixen so clearly. He didn't let his nudity impede him, nor did he stop to find clothes as he strode to his woman.

The nanos questioned his decision. *Logic says we should clothe ourselves and prepare for departure. The enemy is coming.*

The enemy could wait. Touching Lilith couldn't.

She stood stock-still as he stalked her, but when he opened his arms wide, she flew into them, her arms stretching to reach around him.

They hugged, bodies pressing against each other. "I thought I had lost you," she whispered against the skin of his neck.

"Never. We're forever, vixen."

He leaned back enough that he could tilt her chin, bringing her lips into the right angle for him to slant his mouth over them.

As he tasted the sweetness of her mouth, reveled in the closeness of her body, he celebrated even more the twining of their spirits. So what if some of that was their nanos spinning madly around each other. It brought them closer. One mind. One heart.

One kick-ass situation.

He broke the kiss reluctantly, pleased at the flush in her cheeks and the brightness in her beautiful eyes.

"Later," he murmured. "The bots are right about one thing. We need to get moving."

"We are all in danger," she said aloud. "The enemy comes." Or so their bots claimed.

What enemy? He couldn't have clearly said, other than it was an ancient foe and the nanotech advised leaving before it arrived.

We'll see about that. "Okay, all you chosen freaks, time to dry off. The big bad is coming, and we need to be ready."

The nice thing about cyborgs was they didn't argue when the logic was sound.

The next few minutes proved a flurry of naked bodies, as cyborgs, reborn ones, all flesh, no metal, no neural interface, emerged from the pool. All of them chosen by at least one line of nanotech bots—funny how they could react and make decisions as a hive, and yet within that hive, individual splinter groups existed. Every cyborg was chosen by a splinter group, and the bots tuned themselves to their biological choice. From henceforth, they would work only for that host. They'd made their final choice.

But within that vessel, they had room for guests. All of the cyborgs became temporary hosts to passengers, as many as their bodies could hold. The bots, much like pollen from flowers, would hitch rides with whatever they found convenient until they came across fertile ground to adopt.

With so many bots filling them, the cyborgs positively glowed, the sizzle of the nanos dancing on their skin.

Z' looked less than pleased as he tossed robes, which a robot acolyte brought forth, in their directions. "I don't know how you did it. This goes against everything the nanotech ever taught me."

"Times are changing," Avion said as he caught his white robe. "War is coming. The enemy has found us."

"And once again we must run and hide. I know." How weary Z' sounded.

"Or stay and fight." Blow some shit up. Hell yeah.

"We don't have what is needed to win this battle. The ancient nanotech enemy is formidable. As it is, you barely have what you need to escape. Speaking of which, you and your companions should make haste. Your time is short. You must leave while you can."

Lilith touched her mentor's arm. "We can't leave you to fight alone."

"Even though I don't like you, at all," Aramus added, "I wouldn't do that. Give us control of our ship and we'll kick some serious alien ass."

"One cannot prevail against thousands."

The number stunned. "Thousands? Yeah, that's a

couple more than usual."

"The ancient enemy has numbers and weapons the likes of which you cannot imagine. And they are relentless."

"About destroying all the tech? But why?" Avion asked.

On that, neither Z' nor the nanotech would reply.

"Flee to your ship. Flee from here and gather your cyborg brethren. If the ancient enemy has found us, then none of you are safe."

"Are you saying our new homeworld has been discovered?"

"Not yet, but if the *D'zpi* are consorting with humans, then it's only a matter of time before they sell their knowledge of your existence to the ancient ones. The chosen are always hunted, and even the impure will be destroyed."

"Dum-dum-dum," Seth hummed ominously.

"This is no joking matter. You must escape, or else all is lost. You will die."

"Have a little faith, man," Xylo exclaimed. "We're trained soldiers."

"And fantastic lovers." Seth didn't budge as Aramus cuffed him.

"Watch your mouth. There's ladies here."

Eyes glaring at the much diminished pool, Z' muttered, "This is who you've chosen to spread your knowledge?"

"Tell me about it. Men. Such idiots," Anastasia grumbled. "Don't worry. I'll make them see reason. Listen up, idiots, and by that I mean you, husband. You heard the man. We are stupidly outnumbered. Outgunned."

"I, for one, am fine with leaving. Given asshat's initial reception to our presence," Deidra interjected, "I am not inclined to help him too much."

"Now, hold on a second, it's not Z's fault he turned into a crotchety old geezer. I mean look around. It's not like he's had practice making friends lately."

Z's lips tightened. "I have no need of friends."

"And this is why, dude," Seth said, clapping him on the back, "you need to get out of here and get laid."

"The man doesn't need sex but a kick to his metal can." Aramus mimed a boot—which might have held more threat if we wasn't barefoot.

"No sex? Perish the thought," Seth exclaimed. "Everyone needs sex and I, for one, plan to indulge in lots of it once we leave here."

"If you make it out. Which is looking less likely the more time you stand here jabbering. How could the tech possibly think any of you are acceptable hosts?" Z' seemed utterly flummoxed by the concept.

But Avion knew the answer. "Because we are cyborg, and we know how to survive."

CHAPTER EIGHTEEN

Events moved fast, even for someone with nano enhancements like her. One moment Lilith feared for Avion's life, and the next they were running for their lives, heading toward the giant space vessel that would hopefully carry them out of the impending danger zone.

Or at least carry most of them, because not everyone in their group was coming.

Master Z' would not budge.

As unbending as ever, he stood at the bottom of the gangplank, arms folded over his chest, his mien fearsome and, if she were five again, probably intimidating. As a grown woman, she saw it for what it was: a mask. A stoic mask to hide the emotions he kept buried.

"Why won't you come with us?"

"My place is here."

"Here? Here is about to get obliterated."

He didn't deny it.

"You're choosing to die."

He shrugged, his expression still a nonchalant mask. "Perhaps I am. Perhaps I am weary of running and hiding."

"I don't think that's what's tiring you. Yes, maybe you've been playing hide and seek with the nanos' ancient enemy for a long time, but what you're truly hiding from is your emotions. You hide behind the tech and their rules because it's easier than allowing yourself to truly feel. You're choosing the easy way out."

"You think my life is easy?"

"No, but I think you've made your life intentionally complicated in order to forget. But did you ever stop to consider that perhaps you made the wrong choice. Now that I've made the decision to embrace my emotions, the good and the bad, life no longer seems so bleak. I have purpose."

"Because you have found someone. I lost my someone, and no amount of feeling will ever bring her back."

"You say that, and yet you never tried. Never gave yourself a chance to love again."

"Maybe because I didn't want to."

Such a lie. Z' had never tried out of fear of losing again.

I won't be a coward like him. There was a poem she'd once read, *In Memoriam A.H.H.* by Lord Tennyson. It had a line she thought most apt: *'Tis better to have loved and lost than never to have loved at all.*

Despite the risk she took with her emotions, she chose to love.

Avion approached them and placed a hand on her waist. "We need to go. Long-range sensors are detecting an approaching mass."

"The enemy comes, and you must hurry."

"Can we outrun them?" Avion asked.

Z' shook his head. "No, their technology is vastly superior, but you can jump to another galaxy. Your energy crystals were replaced. You have enough power for several jumps. Enough to muddle your trail, gather your brethren and then scatter yourselves across the universe."

"Will we ever be able to stop running?" Avion asked.

"So long as the ancient ones are hunting? No. But, if you are clever, and the nanos seem to think you are, then you will have many planetary revolutions, perhaps centuries of them, before they catch up again."

Xylo stuck his head out of the opening in the

ship and bellowed, "Aramus says to get your fat, silicone asses moving. We've got incoming."

"Go. Now. While you have a chance."

On an impulse, Lilith flung herself at Z' and wrapped her arms around him. This time, he didn't hesitate but hugged her back.

He whispered, "I will deny it if ever asked, but perhaps I was wrong to shut my emotions away. Love is worth every moment you can wring from it."

Then he pushed her away from him in Avion's direction. "Take her and go. Go and don't look back."

Avion snagged her hand and tugged her up the gangplank. At the top, before entering the vessel, she stopped to peer back at Z'.

But he was already gone.

Something they needed to do as soon as possible.

They'd no sooner boarded than the ship's dock door closed behind them. Underfoot, the metal grate floor shivered, and the air hummed as the powerful engines throbbed.

"Come on. We'd better get to our spots. Kentry says we'll be cutting the jump close so Aramus wants all hands on deck."

All decks meant a few key spots. Rosalind, who complained that her new organic eyes weren't as efficient as her bot ones, MJ, and Xylo were assigned to keep an eye on the engine and power generation room. While their knowledge of the ship's systems was incomplete, they could still manage basic repairs should damage occur during their mad dash to achieve the right speed and coordinates to facilitate their jump.

Gearing themselves in flight suits, as an added layer of protection against the harshness of space, Seth and Deidre prepared tool kits and downloaded ship schematics in case they needed to perform emergency repairs. Even the tiniest of holes could rip a ship apart if not taken care of.

Aphelion and Avion were tasked with checking over the fighter jets parked in the hangar for combat. They also took stock of the smaller planet-side crafts. If it looked like they might lose the big ship, then they'd split up and hop into the smaller vessels and shoot off in different directions.

Yeah, as if the cyborgs would run. Somehow, Lilith had a hard time picturing it, although as Avion reminded her, "We might like a good fight, but we enjoy living another day to spite our enemy even more."

Non-soldiers like Laura and Riley had their spots in the medical bay. Being chosen didn't mean the host bodies might not require a bit of patch and repair. While they waited for injuries, that hopefully no one would suffer, the two women also accessed the computers and sifted for any kind of knowledge they could find on just about everything. Okay, maybe not everything, but they were trying to inhale information as fast as they could process it.

Laura was trying to find reports on just what the nanos were capable of. As Seth had shown them with his plastic scheme, not even the tech understood its full potential. The hive might operate in harmony, and yet, the bots themselves, even if they numbered and replicated infinitum, still had branches of individuality. So what one chosen host learned wasn't automatically learned by another. And the one thing none of them could be taught was imagination. It took a human brain for that.

Another thing they couldn't do was just download programming like the military and scientists had done to the cyborgs when they bore the brain computer interfaces. The nanos could absorb at a quick rate, but there was so much to learn, and they ran out of time.

While Laura explored their attributes, Riley spent time examining herself and the fetus she carried.

If I were religious I might call it a miracle.

The first human and cyborg child. Lilith had no knowledge of what would happen to a fetus born of an unenhanced being and a former abomination. Would the child show traces of tech? Should they expose Riley and her unborn infant to the unattached bots they'd taken from the pool and see if it granted them protection?

And more importantly, what would they call the first mixed child?

"Cyman?" Seth suggested. And yes, Lilith giggled at the name.

Especially when Aramus said, "Cyman says eat my fist."

Mirth aside, the pregnancy proved fascinating, even if it raised so many questions. No one knew the answers, and the one person who might have helped them understand had stayed behind.

To die.

Goodbye, Z'. Lilith didn't allow herself to spare too much sadness for him. Z' had made his choice. Just like she'd made hers. She'd chosen her friends—and love.

As for her position during their race to escape? Her place was on the command deck.

Aramus might sit in the control seat and bark orders—lots of them since their mind-to-mind cyborg ability had melted away with their wireless capability—but she was the one with the most knowledge about the ship's abilities. Aramus was counting on her to help him use the vessel's many hidden attributes to aid them in their escape.

Lilith's task, other than info, was to protect them. This wasn't a fight they could win with guns.

In this, Z' was right.

"Kentry, how fucking long until we reach those coordinates?"

"Seven seconds less than the last time you asked," Kentry snarled. The usually composed male tapped furiously at his screens, his brow creased with intense concentration.

At his side, Anastasia sat before her own flashing console, an earpiece in her left ear. Her eyes stared off, unseeing as she concentrated on catching any signs of space chatter.

So far nothing.

There was a moment of stunned silence when the enemy appeared on the edge of their screen, a huge mass of moving darkness, except it wasn't darkness so much as numbers.

Even the usually loquacious and jokester Seth seemed subdued by the army arrayed against them.

Kentry couldn't help but stutter as he announced them. "Counting over a thousand ships, mostly small and rapid scouts, but there are a few bigger ones in there and one fucking planet-sized thing that makes our vessel look like a baby."

"And they are moving fast," Anastasia added, eyes riveted to the screen.

"Fast enough that we might not outrun them. My guess is we should expect their faster attack vessels to reach us while we're still a few minutes out from our target," Kentry grimly announced.

"We'll have to fight," Adam concurred from his spot at the weapons console.

"But not with the small ships. This baby has got an impressive array of outer hull cannons. We're going to have to use them. And with that said, Avion and Seth"—Aramus bellowed loud into the embedded microphone that would relay his orders—"get your asses to battle stations. Deidre and Aphelion, make sure you're ready to run. I need you to manually seal off any leaking sections that don't respond to electronic command."

Wouldn't it figure a pilot would question. "Guns again? But I thought you wanted us ready to fly." Avion didn't quite whine, but he didn't quite manage to miss plaintive.

"No one is going out there. Not unless you want to end up as space jam."

"Sounds messy."

"It is. I need you all on guns and shields. Our only hope is to outrun the majority of the fleet, destroy any fast fliers, and hopefully have this big beauty hold together long enough for us to make a jump."

"Hope? Forget hope," Seth said. "We don't need hope. We're cyborgs. And we don't play to lose."

But they did cut things close.

While they couldn't feel the pull as their vessel hurtled faster and faster to the needed jump coordinates, Lilith kept track of the numbers. Crazy speed. *Whee!* It just wasn't fast enough for the enemy scouts.

A few of them zeroed in on them, not many compared to those ringing the planet they'd left, but enough to cause serious concern.

And provide loads of entertainment.

"Wooo. That's four for me, sukkah!" Adam crowed.

"Brags the guy who's been able to play video games the last few years. I might be rusty, but I'd say my three isn't shabby."

"Bow in awe of my skills," Seth interjected. "Two for the price of one."

Indeed, in true cyborg fashion, machine parts or not, the men turned the situation into a competition. But no matter the joking and rivalry, they were quite deadly and focused. They made the most of the ship's weaponry, ensuring all their shots counted.

It didn't mean they escaped unscathed. The ship was much too big for Lilith to hope to fully shield. However, by letting herself partially merge with the computer—she let her droid nanos travel its electrical paths and subroutines—she could better control the shielding on the outside. Made of energy, it proved challenging to direct because of the way the barrier thickened in areas most at risk of a strike. But it kept them safe.

Until the really big ship caught up to them.

"Holy fuck. What is that thing?" Aramus shouted.

"Really bad," Lilith said. Not a necessary statement. Everyone could tell this wasn't good especially since…

"We are still three minutes from our jump point, but that ship is less than two minutes until they're in firing range."

Their attention on the big ship was disrupted. A bright flash lit their screen. Lilith couldn't help but blink her lids shut. When she opened them, she could see particles rocketing past them as a new minefield was born. A delayed wave of shock swept through space, rattling their massive ship.

"What the hell was that?" Aramus shouted.

That was a planet blowing up. E'dann was no more. Z' and his pool of tech were gone.

Even crazier, the ancient enemy had wiped hundreds of their own out with the explosion. Derelict ships littered space, along with the newly minted asteroid belt.

A foe with no care for its own would show no mercy to them.

But Aramus chose to ignore that with his next request. "Anastasia, I don't suppose they'd answer a hail or a plea for surrender?"

"We can't give ourselves up," Lilith cried.

"No kidding, Goldilocks. I am just seeing if we can try and buy some time."

"I've been trying to connect with them," Anastasia relayed. "But while the phone keeps ringing, they're not answering."

"Fuck." Aramus drummed his fingers on the armrest of his chair, his brow furrowed as he sought a way out of their dilemma.

"I'll take your fuck and multiple it by a holy," Kentry replied.

"Don't tell me there's more bad news."

"Depends on your definition of bad news. There's some kind of massive cannon on the front of their ship that is powering up. According to my analysis, unless we find a way to increase our shield by like a thousand percent, we're space dust."

"Freaky girl, can you increase the shield on the ass end of our ship?"

"I'll do what I can," Lilith said.

"You don't have enough internal energy for that," Anastasia pointed out. "You'll just burn yourself out trying. Maybe we have time to jump before their weapon is fully powered."

Aramus slumped. "We don't." And they all knew it.

They needed more time. She needed to get them more time.

"I can do this." Lilith closed her eyes and reached out to the shields once more. It took only a nudge to focus the shields behind them. All of the force field. She didn't yet add her own kinetic energy to the mix. She'd save that for the last possible second so she could pour as much of herself as she could into it.

Not too much of yourself, vixen. Too much and you might get lost.

But if I don't, she replied, *then it won't matter.*

Funny how she and Avion retained their mental link. She wished she knew why, or how. What made him special? *Is it love that lets our minds speak?*

Arms wrapped around her. "Then we'll become lost together," he whispered.

Kentry announced, "Thirty seconds until the jump, but they're done charging."

"They've fired," Aramus said, followed by the expected, "Fuck. Prepare for impact."

Lilith concentrated, urging all her nanos to help her. *We need your aid if you want to survive.*

Survive. There was a word they didn't argue with even if their very acknowledgement of it meant the bots were more emotionally driven than even they expected. Funny how the instinct for survival trumped all.

Avion and Lilith poured all they had into maintaining the shield, and while it shuddered under the initial impact, it held.

However, the laser burst, a power unlike anything, kept pushing. Their shield wobbled. The ship shuddered.

"I can't hold it," she cried. "I can't—"

She'd forgotten she wasn't alone. Avion was the first to siphon his essence into maintaining their shield. More energy poured into the barrier, as more hums of minds joined. One by one, all the chosen on board, except for Kentry, who kept counting down to death or salvation, became part of the group, pushing back against the laser that would disintegrate them.

Would it be enough? Their collective strength peaked and then wobbled. Lilith sagged in Avion's grasp, and a few of the voices dropped out, their biological hosts tapped out.

It proved enough though. The bright destroyer light blinked off just as Kentry shouted, "Brace yourselves!"

CHAPTER NINETEEN

When they popped out of the jump—what seemed like a blink of an eye but was actually over thirty-two freaking hours—Avion staggered. He didn't fall, though. He couldn't since he also supported a slightly trembling Lilith.

"We did it." She breathed the words, her surprise evident.

"Fucking right we did," Aramus boasted with a smug smile. Yet, he couldn't hide his earlier worry evident by the finger dug grooves in the armrest of his chair. "Kentry, where in space are we?"

"Um, I don't know how, but we're actually only hours from the cyborg homeworld."

"Hours? What do you mean only hours away? How the hell did that happen?" A piercing gaze shot Avion's way, fixing on Lilith who remained cradled in his arms. "Freaky girl, did you mess with my coordinates again?"

Her hair, the tips trimmed into neat ends since they'd met, tickled as they flew with the shake of her head. "Wasn't me. I've never seen these coordinates before."

Aramus frowned. "I have. It's where I was hoping to be able to plot our next course just before we jumped."

No one said it, and yet Avion could have sworn the nanos swarming in Aramus oozed superiority. The confidence of their ornery host was rubbing off on them already.

"Battle stations, report. Any signs of the enemy?"

"Nada. Nothing, zilch," Seth replied, "which

makes me the ultimate winner in our space invader match with nine confirmed hits."

"Rematch later in the simulator?" Adam asked.

"Count me in too, right after I eat a skid full of minerals. I am freaking starving," Avion said, rubbing his flat belly.

As it turned out, they all were hungry. The energy they'd expended, not to mention those lost hours in limbo while they traveled, had their nanos working overtime to ingest. Even the onboard slop proved better than nothing.

"First thing I'm getting Einstein to do," Aramus said as he dumped more salt on his plate, "is fix that bloody food machine so it spits out something edible."

"If that fails, there's a conservatory on board that should be capable of growing some crops," Riley said, playing with her food, a moue of distaste on her lips.

"And we kept some of those beasts those croc dudes were so fond of," Xylo added. "Wanna bet it tastes like chicken?"

With the danger behind them, the cyborgs returned to their usual carefree bantering, some scowling, some smiling, but all together, all individuals and yet part of a family.

A family on its way home. To help them move out.

Avion didn't look forward to the task of telling Joe, who'd worked so hard building the cyborg world, that they needed to vacate. But then again, the ship they'd pirated was huge, the galaxy an even bigger place. They'd find somewhere else to live. Somewhere maybe they wouldn't have to hide or fight.

Okay, they'd still need a little bit of fight because, really, you couldn't take all of a cyborg's fun away.

Speaking of fun.

As couples splintered off, while the singles took

first shift, Avion found himself searching for a room he'd come across while sifting through the ship's schematics.

The holographic chamber was realistic from the shifting sand under their feet to the sound ocean waves made as they rushed up onto the beach and then sucked back down.

It wasn't quite an Earth paradise, not with the three moons in the sky and the pink waters, but it was romantic, and dammit, his vixen deserved it.

After all she'd been through, all she'd done, and given, it was time Avion gave back.

He swept her into his arms and strode to the water's edge.

"Avion, what are you doing?"

"I am going to make love to you in the moonlight." Because he wanted to see the soft kiss of the moons' glow on her skin.

He set her down on her feet, his eyes locked on hers. In silence, they stripped, removing the robes given to them in E'dann's temple. Their bare flesh didn't react to the touch of the air upon it. And yet, she shivered.

Finally Avion could truly appreciate the telling expressions on her face. From the way her lids lowered to half-mast as desire consumed her. The pink flush in her cheeks, which she adorably didn't try and control. The tempting dark buds topping her breasts that begged for his mouth. And, ah, the delicious and shadowy vee between her thighs that promised nirvana.

Enhanced in both strength and agility didn't mean they were graceful as their passion consumed them. In a clash of breath, teeth, and mouths, they came together, joined by the lips, forever tethered by their hearts—and tech souls.

He loved how she let herself go. No attempt to be clinical or in control. On the contrary, Lilith let her knees sag as she lost herself to desire. He caught her before she could fall, and amidst frantic kisses, he lay her down on the warm and damp sand.

"I should have thought to bring a blanket," he murmured against her mouth.

"My nanos can handle a little bit of friction." She nipped his chin before nibbling on his lower lip.

You can handle a little friction? What about a lot? he teased. His body covered hers, his arousal trapped between their bodies. Up she arched, pressing herself closer with a soft moan.

Her silent plea was quite clear. But Avion wasn't ready to give in yet. Despite their frenzied kiss, he let his lips leave hers to trail sensually down her neck, nipping at the soft skin. He stopped for a moment at her pulse.

It fluttered, a rapid staccato against his questing tongue. He kissed it before moving onward. A certain erect tip called him. He answered with his hot mouth, latching onto it and not letting go, even though she cried out and arched.

That's it, vixen. Let yourself feel…

It's too much. She said that, and yet she still grabbed his hair to hold him close.

He switched breasts, grazing his teeth against the hard nub of her nipple. He bit the tip just to hear her scream out his name. "Avion. Please."

"Please what?"

Eyes awash with the mists of heaven met his. "Give me what I need." *Give me yourself.*

I am already yours.

Not what she wanted to hear. He almost chuckled as she growled, "Don't make me kinetic your ass to the ground. I could, you know, and have my way."

For a moment he was tempted to let her try. The idea of her pinning him so that she could straddle and ride him, her hair tossed back, her breasts riding high as she took all of him…

Damn. Another time. This was his seduction.

And she'd just have to wait—and suffer more pleasure.

She wasn't the only one who could use her enhancements for the greater erotic good.

He caught her hands and pinned them to the side, trapping her, despite her struggles.

"How are you doing that? Why are my nanos aiding you instead of me?" she asked as her tech refused to answer.

"Because I promised them an experience they wouldn't forget."

At those words, she stopped squirming. She even stopped breathing. She held herself completely still as his free hand skimmed the length of her smooth thigh. He stopped at the soft curls covering her mound. He cupped her.

She moaned.

He didn't need the sound, though, to know she was aroused. Heat radiated against his hand, and moisture wetted his fingers. He dragged one tip against her and smiled at her shudder. Another finger followed, and he inserted this one between her damp nether lips.

What he truly wanted was a taste, but he doubted he would last that long. His erection throbbed painfully, demanding satisfaction.

He angled himself over her, the head of his shaft probing at the entrance to her sex. Without bidding, her legs parted wide for him, allowing him to nestle his weight between them. It gave him better access as well, and as he captured her lips, he thrust into her. In that moment, he opened his eyes to see her face.

Her lashes fluttered against the tops of her cheeks, she bit her lower lip, and the slightest hint of perspiration dewed her skin.

Such beauty.

Her eyes opened and looked at him.

Such love.

He thrust deeper.

Such pleasure.

I see you. He hummed the words at her.

And she saw him back, saw right into an orgasm that left them both stunned and panting on the holographic sand.

No matter what happened next, they would face it together. "You'll never be alone again." Not so long as he lived.

"Never is a long time."

"Good, because there are so many things I want to do with you."

Starting with a swim, not an intentional one. A wave rolled higher than the rest, soaking them.

"Really rethinking this setting," he grumbled. "What are the chances we can find a towel?"

A soft giggle left her. "About as good as dry clothes."

Sure enough, the robes they'd ditched had gotten a good dousing too. As a matter of fact, they got sucked out from shore into the fake sea.

"Well, it's been a few years since I've done this, but then again, with my new nanos, any experience is good. Ready for your first naked streak up a hall?" he asked as he lifted her to her feet.

"I'm ready for anything."

So was he. He'd faced down death. Found love. And now looked forward to a future.

Even Aramus bellowing through the intercom, "Get some fucking clothes on, you perverts!" couldn't stop his spirit from flying.

I've got love to keep me aloft.

EPILOGUE

Z' stood at the large viewing window, but he didn't actually gaze upon the flowering mountains, the wild blooms slowly bowing under the weight of sifting ash. He didn't react to the explosions that rocked the floor under his feet. Nor did he give the order to evacuate. Not this time.

I tire of running. He tired of living. As guardian of the nanotech, he'd existed much longer than his biological system was ever meant to. Lived long, and alone. A creator with no companion.

Because I lost her.

And instead of dealing with his emotions, he allowed the unfeeling logic of the nanotech to erase them. Except it never completely got rid of his feelings. It simply hid them away where he didn't have to live with them every day.

But Lilith and the others, the cyborgs as they called themselves, they chose to embrace their emotional side. They let the fury of love, anger, need, and friendship guide their actions and thoughts. It should have appalled him. Perhaps, on some level, it did, but only because it forced him to recognize the lack of it in his life.

Happy, angry, or sad, they embodied *life*. And the last hope.

Right or wrong, the cyborgs would be the last carriers of the nanotech. Once the ancient enemy destroyed this planet, Z', along with his pool of creation, would cease to exist. There would be no more quests for candidates. No more trying to seed enhancements along the lesser races. A losing cause as those against the sentient robotic enhancements constantly strove to erase them.

But, while this world might be destroyed today, the tech wouldn't die. The cyborgs would make sure of that.

They are survivors. It was why the bots chose them.

The hosts—with their hundreds of nano passengers—would seed the next generation, an improved version the likes of which Z' never imagined. Because that was the problem. When he locked away his feeling side, Z' had lost his capability to imagine—and hope.

The cyborgs hadn't. Adversity made them stronger. Caring, good or bad, made them more determined. These cyber-enhanced biological beings with individual thoughts and emotions would pioneer a new path, maybe one that would bring them a chance for peace and, at the very least, survival.

A part of him wished he could live to see what chaos and wonders they would leave in their wake on their galactic quest for a true home and a place to belong.

My time is done, though.

A bright light streaked from the sky, its aim unwavering as it headed toward him.

Here comes the end. What would it be like?

Was there a god and a heaven waiting like the humans believed? Did he have a spirit, and would it surf free once he died? Would he find *her* again?

Questions crowded his final thoughts as death zeroed in.

And then he thought no more.

The End of this cyborg series...

But I can't help but wonder if we'll see the cyborgs again. I, for one, would like to know what happens next. What kind of society will the next generation of cyborgs become?

Author's Note: I hope you enjoyed my cyborg saga. If you did, I'd love it if you took a moment and left a review. To check out more of my books, please visit my website at http://www.EveLanglais.com. Thank you for reading. ~ Eve

11863076R00094

Printed in Great Britain
by Amazon.co.uk, Ltd.,
Marston Gate.